**Trust no one, Ian had warned her.**

Gigi quickly stuffed everything back into her backpack and closed it. There were too many reasons for someone to search her house, to follow her home—too many reasons why she might be the key to solving Ian's murder.

But she needed to talk to Hud. She needed to tell him what was happening.

He wanted details? She had plenty of them to share.

And he would listen. Even if he thought it was unbelievable, he would still listen.

He was a good man. He might even be her friend.

Forget that he'd been her fantasy for two years.

The most important detail to her right now was that Hudson Kramer made her feel safe.

D1040960

## Disclaimer

Williams University is a fictional university I've created, loosely based on a conglomeration of campuses and educational facilities in Missouri. I first used it in my book *Kansas City Confessions*, and chances are I will use it again. In this day and age, I didn't think UMKC, Mizzou, Stephens College, Truman State, William Woods and the other fine, real seats of higher learning in my home state would appreciate me creating scenes of murder and mayhem at their schools.

# TARGET ON HER BACK

---

USA TODAY Bestselling Author
## JULIE MILLER

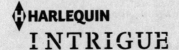

HARLEQUIN
INTRIGUE

In memory of Maggie McGonagall Miller, the gentlest creature I have ever known. What a blessing it has been in our lives that you picked us to be your pack that day at the humane society.

You were so loved, my sweet baby dog. I hope you have squirrels to chase, plenty of treats and a warm lap to snuggle in up in heaven. I miss you.

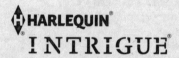

**HARLEQUIN®**
**INTRIGUE®**

Recycling programs for this product may not exist in your area.

ISBN-13: 978-1-335-13644-2

Target on Her Back

Copyright © 2020 by Julie Miller

This edition published by arrangement with Harlequin Books S.A.

For questions and comments about the quality of this book, please contact us at CustomerService@Harlequin.com.

Harlequin Enterprises ULC
22 Adelaide St. West, 40th Floor
Toronto, Ontario M5H 4E3, Canada
www.Harlequin.com

**Printed in U.S.A.**

**Julie Miller** is an award-winning *USA TODAY* bestselling author of breathtaking romantic suspense—with a National Readers' Choice Award and a Daphne du Maurier Award, among other prizes. She has also earned an *RT Book Reviews* Career Achievement Award. For a complete list of her books, monthly newsletter and more, go to juliemiller.org.

### Books by Julie Miller

### Harlequin Intrigue

*Rescued by the Marine*
*Do-or-Die Bridesmaid*
*Personal Protection*
*Target on Her Back*

### The Precinct

*Beauty and the Badge*
*Takedown*
*KCPD Protector*
*Crossfire Christmas*
*Military Grade Mistletoe*
*Kansas City Cop*

### The Precinct: Bachelors in Blue

*APB: Baby*
*Kansas City Countdown*
*Necessary Action*
*Protection Detail*

### The Precinct: Cold Case

*Kansas City Cover-Up*
*Kansas City Secrets*
*Kansas City Confessions*

Visit the Author Profile page at Harlequin.com.

# CAST OF CHARACTERS

*Detective Hudson Kramer*—He doesn't bat an eye when someone calls him half hillbilly or he's teased for being short. He's a fierce protector by nature, and anyone who's actually met the muscular, streetwise detective knows not to mess with him or his badge. But how is he going to handle the shy, leggy redhead from his past who shows up at his crime scene—and has a target on her back?

*Professor Virginia "Gigi" Brennan*—A genius who earned her first degree when most teens were learning how to date, she's smart about equations, not people, and has never been in a relationship. Now the friend who mentored her has been murdered, leaving her with blood on her hands and a scientific mystery to solve.

*Dr. Ian Lombard*—Gigi's boss and mentor saw the genius behind his shy prodigy.

*Tammy Brennan*—Gigi's younger sister got the extrovert genes.

*Gary Haack*—Is Gigi's coworker and fellow professor flirting with her?

*Evgeni Zajac*—A world-class researcher in residence from Lukinburg.

*Hana Nowak*—Evgeni's wife is his translator at the university.

*Kelly Allan*—Gigi's elderly neighbor owns a spoiled Pomeranian named Izzy.

*Dr. Doris Lombard*—Dr. Lombard's widow.

# *Chapter One*

"Let go of me." Professor Virginia Brennan tugged free of the older man's bruising grip. That only made him latch on with both hands.

"Where is Lombard?" The white-haired man's thick accent turned his *w* to a *v* and reminded her of Chekov from the *Star Trek* television show she loved to watch. Only this man was no teen heartthrob or outer space hero.

"I don't know, Dr. Zajac. Bullying me won't help." The chamber music playing in the background beneath the conversations around them sounded oddly discordant as Virginia "Gigi" Brennan found herself backed against the vestibule wall outside the Muehlebach Hotel's grand ballroom.

"You cannot hide him from me," her coworker at Williams University accused.

"I'm not." She shoved at his chest, silently blaming the couple that walked by for averting their heads from the esteemed researcher's harassment and doing nothing to intervene. But Evgeni had seen them, too, and—perhaps wanting to uphold his reputation with the donors who supported his joint research with Ian

Lombard—he released her. Once Gigi slid beyond arm's reach, she gestured to the restroom hallway where she'd last seen her friend and mentor, Ian Lombard. "I saw you two arguing a few minutes ago. Now he's gone." She needed to find Ian herself, so she could leave this nightmare of noise and people at the university reception in downtown Kansas City and go home. Her face ached as she summoned one more PR-worthy smile. "I'm looking for Ian, too. I was really hoping you'd seen him."

Zajac's accent grew more guttural as his anger rose. "He fears me now and will not show his face." He rattled off something in rapid Lukin, speaking too quickly for her to grasp more than "years of research," "betrayal" and something about wrapping his hands around the man's neck.

"I don't know what that means," she said, trying to appease his temper. "Perhaps if you repeat it more slowly." As a visiting professor working on the research team she headed for Ian at Williams University, she knew it was her responsibility to maintain good working relationships with every member of Ian's staff. Evgeni Zajac and his department at their sister university in the tiny Eastern European country of Lukinburg provided the raw materials and several of the preliminary ideas that Ian's team developed into state-of-the-art technology. Keeping both ego-driven men happy was typically part of her job as the calm, quiet wunderkind at the WU School of Engineering and Technology. But she had problems of her own tonight. "I don't suppose you have twenty dollars I could borrow. I need—"

"Where is my Hana?" Evgeni dismissed her with a wave of his hand, spinning around to look for his wife, who also acted as his translator, and he stalked back into the reception room. He cursed his missing wife, Ian and what sounded like the entire North American continent. She had been lectured by temperamental colleagues before, but never in a foreign language. Considering she didn't want to be at this fund-raiser in the first place, and had stayed longer than Ian had promised she'd have to, Gigi figured she didn't need to chase after Dr. Zajac to offer an apology to mend obviously strained international relations.

Clutching her university ID from the lanyard hanging around her neck, she scanned the crowded ballroom for options. She supposed she could ask Gary Haack, another colleague with whom she worked closely on the research team, to loan her the money she'd need for cab fare back to the university where she'd left her wallet, phone and keys. Or maybe he'd call a car for her. How many times had he said he'd like to get closer to her? That she could ask him for anything? About as many times as he'd cornered her in her office or his, invading her personal space in the name of a work issue. She wasn't any good at flirting or being flirted with, so his repeated invitations to one event or another wound up making her feel suspicious rather than flattered. No. Not an option. Knowing Gary, there'd be strings attached to any favor she asked of him. Besides, she couldn't spot his blond head towering over the other guests at any of the catering tables or gathered around the various displays of inventions and technologies Ian, Evgeni and their research team had developed.

Venturing into the crowded room to ask anyone else for help made her almost physically ill. She'd come with Ian tonight, and now Ian was gone. Getting herself home was all on her shoulders now.

She slipped away from the party and retrieved the old ivory sweater she'd thrown on at the last minute from the coat check room. Sliding it on for warmth over the short sleeves of her black sequined dress, and hugging it around herself for the comfort of her late mother's memory since she'd knit it for her years ago, Gigi took the escalator up to the lobby. She paused at the bank of glass doors facing Wyandotte Street and exhaled a weary sigh.

Of course. It was raining. The sidewalk outside was wet and shiny, reflecting the lights from traffic, the hotel and Municipal Plaza across the street. Even if the weather was nice and she wasn't a woman alone late at night, the university would be too far to walk from here, especially in the black high heels that pinched her toes.

*Options, Gigi. Think of options.* Going back to that crowd and begging someone for help wasn't one of them.

Thinking was what she excelled at when she wasn't overwhelmed by people and emotions, and when she saw the bright lights from the city bus letting out passengers at the corner of Twelfth Street and Wyandotte, she knew what to do.

Flipping over her university ID, she let out an audible breath. Her bus pass was still tucked inside the plastic sheath. Clutching the lanyard in her fist, she stepped out into the chill of the rainy autumn night. With her heels splashing over the pavement, she hurried across the street and knocked on the closing bus doors so she could climb in before it drove away.

Twenty minutes later, having used up every bit of extroverted energy her shy genes could muster, she was back on campus. She was tired, damp and cold. But she still wasn't getting home anytime soon.

She cleared her throat, giving the night security guard in the gray-and-black uniform another chance to wake up.

"Officer Galbreath?" she repeated, hugging her long cardigan over her dress. It was colder here inside the regulated air of the Williams University Technology Building than it had been outside, perhaps because her feet were still wet and squishing in her ruined shoes. "Jerome?"

Her only reply was a gravelly snore. The older gentleman with the mahogany skin and salt-and-pepper hair had dozed off at his desk in the lobby. Since she'd been absentminded enough to leave her university ID looped around her neck like a piece of jewelry, she had her own key card to enter the research lab on the second floor. But if Jerome Galbreath didn't log her in before she did so, she'd set off the after-hours security alarm the moment she opened the door.

The last thing she wanted was for campus security and the Kansas City police to swarm the building and question why she was breaking into the lab in this ridiculously short and soggy getup, long after classes had ended for the day and most of the campus had shut down for the weekend. Gigi hated swarms of anything—birds, bugs, people crowding around her, too many people talking at once.

Tonight's party had been pure torture. She'd done the job the university had expected of her, but now she needed solitude and silence to take the edge off her frayed nerves. That meant yoga pants or jammies, a cup of hot tea and a book or movie to immerse herself in at home.

Only, she couldn't get home.

She already felt like a dork for leaving her phone, keys and wallet in her backpack at work because she'd been so nervous about attending the hoity-toity reception at the Muehlebach Hotel. *Come to the party, Gigi,* Dr. Lombard had said. *Put on something pretty. Ride in the limo with me to the hotel and drink champagne. The university is buying. You deserve to have a little fun to celebrate our success. You do have a party dress, don't you?*

Um, no.

It wasn't until Dr. Lombard had said that he needed her to come along to explain the technicalities of their research to interested guests while he schmoozed the crowd of visiting Lukinburg dignitaries and donors who'd made generous contributions to the department that she'd agreed to go. He needed her expertise to make tonight a success.

That had always been her Kryptonite—someone needing her. Since most people, beyond her sister and a few close friends, barely noticed her shy, studious self, the idea of being important enough to be needed, to be necessary to another person, was as alluring as it was unfamiliar. She'd been suckered in by those words more than once in her life. As smart as she was, it was a lesson she should have learned by now.

A lesson that wouldn't leave her stranded in downtown Kansas City after dark.

She was more than eager to support Ian Lombard's cutting-edge research into new-market computer-component and power-consumption applications, and the Lukin investors were willing to fund that research because it gave them a market for the raw materials produced in their country. Gigi knew how to conduct herself in a classy manner at sedate university functions, how to smooth things over for her brilliant, but volatile boss. And although she'd gotten lost during Dr. Zajac's tirade, she even spoke a few words of Lukin, so she could communicate with their guests on a rudimentary level. She was proud of Dr. Lombard's work—her work, too, since she'd been his right hand for two years now. She'd taken over teaching one of his classes to free him up to concentrate on fast-tracking his research.

But celebrate? Schmooze? Dr. Gigi Brennan fit that role about as well as this fancy dress she'd borrowed from her younger, curvier sister fit her. Although Tammy had insisted that she couldn't go wrong with a little black dress, the outfit was too short to be comfortable and hung loose on Gigi's willowy frame.

Gigi's willingness to put on Tammy's dress and brave the reception had ended the moment she realized Dr. Lombard had left the party without her. He'd needed her, all right—to cover for his inexplicable absence, to represent the department while he went off and…what? Went home to get a full night's sleep? Skyped a phone call with his drama professor wife who was currently researching Henrik Ibsen in Scandinavia? Rendezvous in a hotel room upstairs with one of those dewy-eyed grad students he liked to flirt with while said wife was out of the country?

The why didn't matter. Gone was gone. Lombard had taken advantage of her inability to say no to him. She'd call her sister for a ride, but Tammy had been at a teachers' conference in Vegas this week and was staying a couple of extra days to have some fun. Gigi was on her own. Nothing new there. She should be used to that by now.

Gigi had made it back to the university where her car was parked.

But she wasn't going any farther without her keys.

And a sleeping security guard.

She was the responsible one. The family bread-winner who'd stepped up to take custody of her underage sister after their parents had died in a traffic accident. She kept food on the table and a roof over her and Tammy's heads.

So what if she got so caught up in her work some days that she lost track of the time?

So what if she babbled like an idiot or completely shut down when her nerves got the better of her?

*She* was the one with the Ph.D. she'd earned by her twenty-fourth birthday three years earlier.

*She* was the one who'd been selected to be a part of Dr. Lombard's team to find applications for his technology. Weaponry. Environmental sciences. Medical programs. Business efficiency models. There was a lot of money to be made in the practical applications of Lombard's research. Money meant not just an impressive paycheck for the duration of his funding, but also the prestige that would allow her to move to a bigger university, like Massachusetts Institute of Technology or Harvard, to pursue her own research, or at least to head up her own program here in Kansas City.

With a résumé like that, she should be able to get herself home.

Gigi adjusted her glasses on her nose and silently debated how difficult it would be to extract the computer tablet from beneath Jerome's folded arms on top of the desk where he slept. She quickly dismissed that idea because the guard wore a gun, and if she accidentally startled him awake, who knew how he'd react? For a split second, he might think she was stealing the tablet, or worse, attacking him, reacting before his thoughts cleared enough to recognize her.

So, she knocked on the counter above the desk. When he stirred, she reached over the counter to nudge his arm. "Jerome?"

She jumped back half a step when the guard's breathing stuttered. Flattening his palms atop the desk, he pushed himself up in his chair and blinked her into focus.

"Professor Brennan?" He picked up the nearly empty coffee mug on the desk beside him, frowning before he set it back down and pushed it away. "That didn't do me any good. Don't know why I'm dragging tonight. Looks like you got caught out in that rainstorm."

"I did. Thankfully, it didn't last long." She pushed a lock of wet auburn hair that stuck to her cheek up into what was left of the bun she wore at her nape. "I'll dry out soon enough."

He smiled up at her for a moment before squeezing his eyes shut and rubbing at his temple. "Can't seem to stay awake."

Gigi leaned against the counter, worried about the lines furrowed beside his eyes. "Are you feeling all right?"

"I've got a mother of a headache. Maybe I'm coming down with something."

Gigi's Ph.D. was in applied physics, not medicine, but even she could see that something was off about the man who'd worked the night shift here since retiring from KCPD, a few years even before she had joined the faculty. Jerome Galbreath didn't just fall asleep on the job. "I've got a couple of ibuprofens up in my office. Would that help?"

"Maybe. Thanks." Still seeming a little disoriented, Jerome inspected the imprint that the corner of his computer tablet had left on his hand before shaking off the drowsy fog. "How long was I out?"

"I've only been here a few minutes. Friday nights are pretty slow. I imagine it can get kind of boring."

He shook his head, disagreeing with her speculation. "I didn't just doze off. That was a deep sleep. Sorry about that." He punched the power button on the tablet and pulled up the personnel screen. A lot of expensive equipment and cutting-edge technology was housed in the lab where she worked on the second floor. Only a handful of professors and staff held key cards to access the faculty offices and lab itself, and the university kept close tabs on anyone who entered the building. Officer Galbreath rose to his feet and pushed the tablet across the countertop so she could sign in. Even as he rubbed his temple again, he offered her his usual smile. "You're here mighty late."

"I left my bag up in my office when I changed for the party." If Dr. Lombard hadn't been in such a hurry to put in an appearance at the reception, she might have remembered to borrow an evening purse from Tammy, too, and switch a few necessary items to it. Like car keys and her phone.

"Do you have your key card?"

Gigi pulled the purple-and-white Williams University lanyard she wore from inside the front of her dress and held up the attached key card ID. "Right here."

"Doesn't exactly go with your outfit," Jerome teased.

"That's why I'm not the fashion icon of the family." She scrolled through the names on the screen to find her own but frowned when she saw the one that was still highlighted. "Is Dr. Lombard here?"

Surely, he wasn't here at this hour to work. Unless that argument she'd witnessed between Ian and Dr. Zajac had prompted him to come back to the lab to... what? Retrieve evidence to prove a theory or show proof of a patent? Correct a mistake in their findings or investigate a flaw in their product development?

The security guard took the tablet from her and frowned. "I must have forgotten to log him out when he left."

"But he was here?" Gigi clarified. "When?"

"He was in a meeting in his office when I came on duty at nine. There was a message on my desk saying he wasn't to be disturbed." He punched in a number on his phone before handing her a folded-up note. "I thought he had that reception with those foreign investors."

Gigi nodded, skimming the brief, typed missive. "I was there with him. For a while."

> *Jerome—*
> *Private meeting in my office tonight.*
> *No visitors. No calls.*
> *I'll lock up.*
> *Dr. Lombard*

Private meeting? Tonight? When he should be out celebrating his success? And not leaving her stranded? She was Ian's right hand when it came to work. Why wouldn't she know about this meeting?

Maybe she should rethink the curvy young student theory. "You didn't see anyone with him, did you?" Although the sterile lab was hardly conducive to romance, Ian did have a leather couch in his office. "A woman, perhaps?"

"I didn't even see him. Probably my mistake, and he's long gone." Jerome grinched about not being old enough to nod off like he had and hung up the phone. "He's not answering in his office." Gigi went ahead and signed herself in and Jerome waved her around the counter and connected the chain from his desk to the outer wall to indicate that access to the building was blocked while he was away. "I'll walk up with you and make sure he's gone before I sign him out. It's past time for me to make rounds, anyway."

Jerome opened the elevator doors and ushered her inside. When the doors opened again onto the second floor, the hallway was dark except for the security lights casting a sickly yellowish glow across the white marble floor tiles. The entire wall across from them was devoted to the research lab and faculty offices behind a row of floor-to-ceiling windows framed by stainless steel and secured by key-card access locks. The impressive facade allowed students and visitors to peek inside without disturbing the pristine sterility of the workstations where Gigi and Ian, other university staff, visiting professors, and promising graduate students worked. The display of technology was also meant to inspire students in classrooms on this side of the hallway, as well as motivate visiting donors to give even more money to the university and its research-and-development programs.

But tonight, instead of inspiring or motivating or even feeling much like the familiar workplace she was used to, the darkened lab on the other side of the glass was filled with shadows. The vague outlines of tables and equipment took on menacing forms at night, like predators in a cave, lying in wait for their unsuspecting prey to wander inside to become dinner. All her imagination needed were a few blinking monitor lights to masquerade as eyes for the creatures, and the nightmare crawling over her skin and raising goose bumps would be complete.

Gigi startled at the brush of Jerome's hand against her arm. "Sorry."

She pushed aside his apology and stepped off the elevator. "My fault. I was letting my imagination get carried away with how creepy this place looks at night." She followed Jerome across the hall, pulling her key card from around her neck as he unhooked the flashlight from his belt and shone it through the glass.

"It's mighty dark in there," Jerome pointed out. "I can't tell if Dr. Lombard's office door is open from here, but there sure isn't any light coming from there."

Gigi swiped her card through the lock, but nothing happened. "That's strange." She thought again of the shadowy predators inside. "There aren't even any equipment lights glowing…" When her card failed to work a second time, she typed in her override code and opened the door. She paused, grabbing Jerome's arm as he entered ahead of her. This wasn't right. "There should be lights on. Monitors regulating electricity. Ongoing tests."

Jerome nodded and flipped the light switch beside the door. Nothing. He went to the nearest table and turned the manual switch on a lamp. No light. "Do you think we blew a fuse?"

She glanced up at him. "We don't use fuses anymore. The lab and research offices are on a self-contained, computer-regulated system."

His blank stare told her she'd missed the point. "Figure of speech, Professor."

"Oh. Right." Her trepidation turned to concern about the stability of the millions of dollars of sensitive equipment housed here. "The lab is on its own breaker box from the rest of the building, including security. A surge of some kind must have blown the entire circuitry. Otherwise, the backup protocols would have engaged." She shook her head. "Nothing's on in here."

"Take this." Jerome handed her his flashlight. "I've got a light on my phone. I'll go down to the basement and check the breakers. Will you be all right in here by yourself?"

Gigi nodded, turning the light to her closed office door near the front of the lab. "Everything I need should be in my backpack."

Jerome hesitated a moment, surveying the dark cavern around them, including Ian's closed door. "Apparently, Dr. Lombard did leave. Why wouldn't he check himself out?"

"Maybe he didn't want to wake you." Gigi offered him a silent apology. "You *were* sleeping on your tablet."

"I worked the night shift at KCPD for twenty years before I took this position. I have never fallen asleep on the job. Not like that." His eyes narrowed as he considered an idea. "Will you be able to find your way downstairs okay? Once I reboot the system, I want to go back to my desk and smell my coffee."

"Smell your coffee?" She swung her light right into his face. He squinted and put up his hand against the brightness before she quickly lowered the beam. "Sorry. Your headache."

"Exactly." He lowered his hand. "Call it an old policeman's hunch."

Gigi pretended she understood what he was talking about, even as her brain started calculating possible explanations. "You go ahead. As soon as I get my bag and keys, I'm heading home."

"Okay." His face softened with a wide grin. "Be sure to check with me on your way out. I don't like losing track of people."

"I'll bring the ibuprofen down when I do." She turned to her office and took a couple of steps around a stainless steel table before her deductive mind finally got what he'd meant by his odd comment. "Wait. Do you think your coffee was drugged...?"

By the time she reached the hallway, Jerome had already disappeared into the elevator. Gigi shook her head, realizing that solving one mystery had led to another. "Why drug that sweet old man?"

Maybe she was too tired, too drained from all the social interaction of the evening to fully understand anything tonight. She turned the light to her office door and made her familiar way through the maze of equipment to unlock it and head inside. She instinctively flipped on the light switch inside the door, then silently chided her foolishness when nothing turned on. She retrieved her backpack from her desk before opening the center drawer and tucking the bottle of pills for Jerome into a side pocket. She swapped out the flashlight for the reassurance of her own phone in her hand and turned on the flashlight app. Then she looped the bag over one shoulder and headed back to the lab.

Metal clanged against metal and she froze. Had the shadowy predators awakened? "Stupid imagination," she muttered. She swept her light across the lab, although it wasn't bright enough to reach every corner.

She'd heard one sharp clank, then nothing. Was someone here? "Jerome?" No way could he have gotten down to the basement and back so quickly. But was that…? She squeezed her eyes shut, as if that would sharpen her hearing. Was that someone breathing? Gasping? Her eyes popped open again. Now the only thing she heard was her pulse throbbing in her ears. She wasn't alone. "Ian? Are you here?"

She pulled her door shut and turned toward Ian's office at the back of the lab. She'd gone five steps when her hip smacked into the corner of a cart that had rolled out of place. Ignoring the stinging bruise that was already forming, she moved the cart back into its proper position and stepped around it. "Ian?"

Was that what she'd heard? The cart bumping against a table? She knew enough about physics—a lot about physics—to know that the cart hadn't just moved on its own. Had they had a break-in? Was that why someone would drug Jerome? Why the lights would be out? She quickened her steps, watchful for any other carts jumping out to attack her. There didn't seem to be anything missing. Although she could imagine Ian had brought his latest conquest here to his office, and they'd knocked into tables and equipment trying to get at each other, unable to keep their hands to themselves until they made it into the privacy of his office. At least, that's what she imagined a truly passionate encounter to be like. Losing track of space and time, knocking into things, laughing, touching, loving…

Gigi shook those longing thoughts out of her head and concentrated on the facts. A clandestine meeting wouldn't require flipping the circuit breaker—or drugging the security guard who had no reason to question Ian entering the building, with or without a guest.

"Ian? I'm sorry to interrupt your meeting, but if you're here, answer me."

Her shoe crunched over broken glass and she stopped. Her blood chilled away that brief shot of annoyance and left fear in its wake. "Ian?"

Something was wrong. Ian might have a weakness for a pretty face, but his pride in his work, maintaining a state-of-the-art showplace and feeding his ego, took second place to nothing and no one. Something was very wrong. "Ian!"

She slid on something slippery and she grabbed a nearby table for balance. This was not good. She pulled her foot up from the goo she'd stepped in, hating the gross, sucking sound it made.

Righting herself against the table, she turned her light to the puddle of red on the floor. A soupy brown liquid coated the top of it. Was that a chemical spill? She couldn't identify the faint acrid smell that stung her nose. The lab had been in pristine condition when she'd left for the reception. Ian would never allow a mess like this. "Dr. Lombard? Are you in here?"

All at once, the lights kicked on, blinding her momentarily before she blinked her surroundings into focus. Now the damage was clear. She was walking over jagged shards of glass stained with… "Blood."

She gasped a fearful breath. "Oh, my God. Jerome!" She shouted an alarm for the security guard to return. "We had a break-in!"

As if she could yell loudly enough for him to hear

her through steel beams and cinder blocks. Gigi didn't wait for the guard to come to her rescue. There'd been a struggle here. And someone was hurt.

"Dr. Lombard!"

For a split second she hoped that whoever belonged to this trail of blood had gotten himself to a hospital. But then she heard the sounds coming from Ian's office. Something falling to the floor. Groans. Curses. Another crash. "Ian!" Gigi punched in 911 and skirted her way around the blood to reach Ian's office. "Ian? Are you here? Are you all right?"

He wasn't.

She shoved open the door, dropping her bag to the floor before she raced across the room and knelt beside her boss. "Oh, my God. What happened?"

Ignoring her attempt to get him to lie flat on the floor, he flung his arm up to pull a stack of books off his desk. He cried out when they hit his stomach and fell to the floor. A crumpled notepad dotted with blood lay on the floor next to him, the blood soaking into the paper and blotting out some of the numbers and symbols written there. He pushed away Gigi's hands and flopped what seemed to be his one functioning arm at the desk again, pulling more things onto himself and the floor.

"Ian, stop. Lie still." She pushed him onto his back, trying not to gag at the wounds puncturing his tuxedo shirt and turning the white pleats red. He was hurt badly, maybe dying. "What do you need?"

"Pen," he muttered, spitting blood when he made the *p* sound. "Find…finish…"

The dispatcher had answered her call and was talking to Gigi on the phone. But she ignored the questions and pulled down a pen from the top of his desk. She pressed it into his hand and tugged a velour throw blanket off the nearby couch, wadding it up to press it against the worst of his wounds. He was weak, but struggling with her, determined to scribble something on the paper beside him.

Gigi punched the speaker button on her phone and set it on the desk, freeing her hands to stanch his wounds. But there were so many. There was so much blood. "Ian? Stay with me."

"Ma'am?" The dispatcher's voice was louder now. "Tell me what's happening. Are you all right?"

Shoving at her glasses to keep them from falling off her nose, Gigi leaned over Ian. She shouted to the dispatcher. "I'm okay. My boss…" She swallowed her panic. She needed to make sense. "There's been a break-in at the Williams University Technology Lab. My boss, Ian Lombard, he's been stabbed. He's bleeding badly."

So much blood. She could see now that the pool of blood she'd stepped in earlier had become a trail of red dots across the carpet in here, and then a smear that led right to Ian's desk. He must have been attacked out in the lab, then made his way in here to call for help or to escape his killer or to… "Damn it, Ian, stop messing with that paper."

"I've dispatched an ambulance and the police to your location. Ma'am? I need your name. Can you tell me your name?"

"Virginia Brennan. My friends call me…" She stopped that useless sentence and wiped the perspiration from Ian's forehead before returning the pressure to his wounds. Not that she could cover them all. But she had to try. "Professor Virginia Brennan. I work with Dr. Lombard. Please hurry."

The blood was coating his lips now, trickling from his mouth as he tried to say something to her. "Safe…"

"Who did this to you?" Gigi tried to decipher his babble. At least he'd given up on writing his last will and testament or whatever note had been so important that he'd risked his life to put pen to paper instead of calling an ambulance himself. "He's been stabbed multiple times," she reported to the dispatcher. "Abdomen and chest. He's losing a lot of blood."

"Is the victim awake? Responsive?"

"Must finish…work…" he spat out. "Go…"

"I'm not going anywhere," she promised before answering the dispatcher. "He's conscious. But he's incoherent. Ian, I don't understand—"

With a strangled gasp, he grabbed a hank of her long hair and jerked her down to gasp in her ear. "Finish it."

"Finish what? What are you talking about? You're not finished."

He rolled his head from side to side. "Made deal… But I couldn't… So sorry…"

"Sorry for what? What deal?" His life was seeping through her fingers.

"My prize…" His rheumy eyes tried to focus. "Too damn…smart… Smarter…than me."

"Don't talk. Save your strength." She cursed the urge to cry and extricated his fingers from her hair to speak to the dispatcher. "There are too many wounds. I can't stop all the bleeding."

"I thought she…my own fault… You must…"

"An ambulance is on its way."

"Listen to me!" Fluid bubbled up from his lungs and Gigi's eyes burned with tears. Help wouldn't get here in time. Where was Jerome? Where was that stupid ambulance? "Take…" He wadded up the paper he'd scribbled all over and, with a monumental effort, dragged his hand onto his stomach, nudging it into her blood-stained fingers. "For you… Trust no one…" She glanced down at the words that were so important to him and saw nothing but random letters and numbers. "Finish…"

"Finish what?" Gigi whipped her gaze around the room, desperate for help. "Help me!"

"You'll…understand…"

"Understand what?" When he kept batting against her hand, she took the paper and stuffed it into the pocket of her sweater. But even in those few seconds that she'd eased the pressure on his wounds, his eyes drifted shut. "No! Ian!"

She patted his cheek, urging him to open his eyes again, mindless of the bloody fingerprints she left on his skin. "Stay with me."

But he was gone.

Ian Lombard was dead.

Gigi sat back on her heels, eyeing her soiled hands, feeling the tears burn down her cheeks. She heard someone hurrying through the lab behind her. Help. At last. "In here!" She turned her head, catching a shadowy movement from the corner of her eye. "Jerome—"

Pain exploded in her skull. Her glasses flew off and she crumpled to the floor beside the dead man. The room spun and blackness consumed her.

## Chapter Two

"Whose honor were you defending this time?"

Detective Hudson Kramer touched his bruised knuckles to his lips, wiping away the blood that trickled down his unshaven chin, and gave his amused partner the stink eye. He stepped away from the two dazed men lying in a puddle on the asphalt. "Make yourself useful and get out your handcuffs."

At least Keir Watson had had the good grace to even the odds in this lame excuse for a back-alley brawl behind the Shamrock Bar where Hud had been plying his dubious charm on a pretty blonde. He'd had about twenty minutes of doing all right for a thirty-two-year-old whose only luck with women was the bad kind. Twenty minutes of thinking he wasn't going straight to the friend zone and that she might just say yes if he asked her out on a real date and kissed her good-night. Twenty minutes of sharing laughs and feeling like his luck just might be changing until Stinky Smith here and his wingman, I'm-With-Stupid Jones, decided that loud and drunk and hitting on anything with boobs was going to get them laid tonight.

Hud had been content to let the bartender handle

the rowdy pair—a bar frequented by local cops rarely needed a bouncer on duty—until Smith and Jones had lurched over to his table, sat down on either side of Ricki and proceeded to horn in on the blonde and her drink. Hud had politely asked the two drunks to leave. But *polite* had no effect on their beer-soaked brains, and when one of them draped his arm around Ricki and her smile turned to a look of panic, Hud stepped up to get the job done.

"I identified myself as a cop," Hud assured his friend, hauling the guy who'd taken a swing at him to his feet. Although polar opposites in dress and demeanor, Keir Watson was as close to Hud as his own brother—the entire Watson clan made Hud feel like part of the family, especially now that his own siblings had found their hearts' desires away from Kansas City. So, he took great pleasure in flicking at the grime that dusted the damp lapel of Keir's preppie suit before pulling his own cuffs out of the back pocket of his jeans and slapping them on the bruiser with more muscles than brains. "I escorted these gentlemen out the back door, offered to call a cab for them, warned them I'd cite them for drunk and disorderly..." He cinched the cuff around Stinky's other wrist, securing them without being too tight. He looked up into Stinky's unfocused eyes, making sure the young man understood they were going for a walk. "Then this bozo thought taking a swing at me was a good idea."

Hud had stopped growing when he hit five foot eight. Despite his lack of height, a combination of martial arts and weight training often gave him an advantage over larger opponents in a fight. Besides, he didn't have to be as street smart as life and his years as a detective with KCPD made him in order to out-wit these two.

"But you escorted them out of the bar because…?" Keir was still trying to push his buttons as he followed Hud with his prisoner. They escorted them to the end of the alley where a uniformed officer would meet them with a black-and-white to drive the two perps down to the precinct to sleep off their out-of-control drunkenness. "I know there's a woman involved."

"Give it a rest, Keir. Jesse the bartender cut them off, and they got a little surly. When I asked for their ID, they started to raise a ruckus. I was not counting on…" Hud bit back a curse when his prisoner weaved to the side, doubling over to retch behind a row of trash cans that had been knocked over in their scuf-fle. "You okay, bud? Feeling better?"

"Yeah," Stinky drawled. Feeling a touch more sober, he stopped and tried to take stock of his sur-roundings. "Where's Danny? He didn't make it with that blonde, did he?"

Danny must be the guy in the prophetic I'm With Stupid T-shirt. He perked up at the mention of his name. "What blonde? Did I get her number?"

Keir laughed. "I knew there'd be a blonde. Now this little fracas is starting to make sense." He grinned at Hud. "They said something crude. You took ex-ception. When you asked them to leave, they didn't cooperate. So, you *encouraged* them to do so. Is that about right?"

Hudson grumbled a curse at just how well his part-ner knew him.

They cleared the alley and headed toward the circle of light beneath a lamppost to wait for the black-and-white to pull up. "What's your friend's name, Danny?" Keir asked.

"Kyle." Danny stumbled as he tried to turn and get a look at the detective in the suit and tie. "Who are you?"

"I'm the police, Danny. Detectives Watson and Kramer. Remember?" Keir's patience in explaining the situation to the two men who likely wouldn't remember much of this encounter made Hud shake his head. "You're both going to spend the night in jail. You understand that, right?"

"Am I drunk?" Kyle asked, staggering ahead of Hud.

"Yep," Hud assured him. When they reached the lamppost, he turned the young hotshot so he could sit on the concrete barrier beside it. "You're going to be a little sore in the morning. I had to twist your arm and put you down on the ground to get you to stop trying to hit me."

"I hit you?"

"Lucky punch," Hud conceded.

"Did Danny hit you?"

"I doubt it," Keir answered, helping Danny sit before he fell. "He'll be a little sore, too. He tripped over the two of you and face-planted the asphalt before I could catch him."

Kyle appeared to be nodding off. Hud gently tapped his cheek to force his bleary eyes open. "You don't talk to a lady like that again. You don't touch her unless you have permission. You don't drink so much you can't even tell me your name. And you sure as hell don't get behind the wheel of a car when you're like this." Hud reached around Kyle and pulled his wallet from his jeans. "Let's try this one more time. I'm Detective Kramer, KCPD. I'm going to check your ID. You got any weapons, sharp objects, drugs on you?"

"I don't think so." Kyle answered while Hud read his name off his license. "Are you going to arrest me?"

"For being a dumb ass?" He tucked the billfold into Kyle's chest pocket as a pair of uniformed officers pulled up in their vehicle. "You're not worth the paperwork. Just be safe. And be smarter about how much you're drinking next time."

After the uniforms drove away with the two drunks, Keir stepped back into the end of the alley beside him. "So you got those two idiots safely out of the bar and off the streets. How'd you make out with the pretty blonde they were so rude to?"

Hud swore again. "Ricki. I left her alone." He checked his watch as he retreated toward the Shamrock's back door. "I've been gone twenty-five minutes. You got this?"

He barely saw Keir's nod before he ran back inside the Shamrock. By the time he cleared the polished walnut bar with its green vinyl seats and zeroed in on the empty table where he'd left Ricki, there was no point in hurrying. The only thing he could cuddle up with there was his worn leather jacket. A quick scan of the remaining patrons at the tables and pool tables told him his "date" had left.

He turned to the bearded bartender in the leather vest, hoping Jesse Valentine would tell him she'd just stepped into the ladies' room. Jesse gave him an apologetic smirk. "Sorry, man. She got on her phone almost as soon as you went outside with the Blunder Twins. A guy showed up about five minutes ago. She left with him."

Propping his hands at his waist, Hud tipped his face to the tin-tiled ceiling and let the suckage of this particular Friday night wash over him. He'd often been the friend his sisters or another woman called for that safe ride home. The irony of being the man the woman no longer wanted to hang out with wasn't lost on him.

He startled at Keir's hand on his shoulder before his partner pulled him back to the bar. Keir asked for a glass of ice water. He dipped his handkerchief inside and handed it to Hud to press against his mouth. "Everything all right?"

"You know, I gave up the prime of my dating life to raise my younger brother and sisters." Hud perched on a stool and held the cold cloth to his split lip. "I don't regret it for one second. We needed each other after Mom and Dad died. I was going to keep the family together, no matter what. But now they've all got college degrees and careers. They're engaged or married and starting families, and I can't catch a break with a woman now that I'm available and ready for some action."

"Ready for some action? Seriously?" Keir pulled out the stool beside him but waved off Jesse's offer of his regular drink. "Please don't tell me that's a line you've used."

"Don't judge me."

"You've got no game, my friend."

"Tell me about it."

"Seriously, dude." Keir clapped him on the shoulder to take the sting out of his words. "If she stood you up while you were taking care of business, then she's not the one for you."

Small comfort. Lonesome was lonesome. And Hud had spent far too many nights on his own or with a woman who wasn't the one for him.

The fact that Keir had ventured out into the earlier rainstorm on their night off and wasn't drinking pricked at Hud's suspicions, giving him a respite from his pissy mood. It was no coincidence that his partner had come to the Shamrock looking for him. Something must be up at work, especially since he had a beautiful wife and baby girl waiting for him at home. Hud pulled out his wallet and asked Jesse how much he owed for the warm, half-drunk beers at his table.

"They're on the house," the bartender assured him, refusing his money. "Thanks for clearing out the riff-raff."

There were any number of things he'd rather be doing tonight than working, and all of them had to do with a woman. But since there were none in his life, he turned his attention to his partner. If something was wrong with the family, Keir would have mentioned it right away. This was KCPD business. Hud pushed to his feet and pocketed Keir's soiled handkerchief before crossing the noisy bar to his table. "Why aren't you home with Kenna making goo-goo eyes at that new baby of yours? I know you didn't drop by just to back me up with Stupid and Stupider."

Keir followed. "That *new* baby is six months old

and you haven't visited your goddaughter in two weeks, Uncle Hud."

His mood brightened by the mention of his goddaughter. Hud grinned as he tucked in his flannel shirt and adjusted the gun holstered on his belt. "Lilly's eyes still as blue as the sky?"

"Now that's the line you ought to use," Keir teased. "She's as beautiful as her mother. Just as headstrong, too."

Hud pictured Keir's wife, a former criminal defense attorney turned county prosecutor who enjoyed the well-earned professional nickname, The Terminator, and laughed. "I bet she is. Hey, if you and Kenna need a night out on your own, all you have to do is call Uncle Hud, and I'd be happy to come babysit that sweet little angel."

"I will take you up on that offer," Keir said. "But not tonight."

"I take it we caught a case?"

Keir nodded. "Murder. One of the professors over at Williams U was found dead in his lab. Multiple stab wounds. B shift is short staffed, and this is a high-profile enough victim that the captain wants us to get the investigation started ASAP."

"High profile?" Hud shrugged into his jacket, his personal life pushed aside at the urgency of those first few hours in a murder investigation.

"It might be related to that bombing we had downtown this past summer."

"When the Lukinburg royalty was in town?"

Keir nodded. "The professor's lab is funded by the Lukin government. Not sure if the two incidents are related, but Captain Hendricks wants us to check it out. You up to working on a Friday night?"

"Well, I'm not going home to snore in my recliner, watch TV and feel sorry for myself."

"Good man. I'll drive." Keir buttoned his jacket and headed for the door.

Hud tossed a tip on the table for the waitress and followed his partner out into the night. "Works for me."

FORENSIC EVIDENCE WAS in plentiful supply at the crime scene. But it was up to Hud, Keir and the crime lab to make sense of it.

While the medical examiner rolled the victim to the elevator in a body bag, Hud pulled a pair of disposable foot covers over his work boots and squatted down to inspect the broken glass and paperwork tossed around the pool of blood in Ian Lombard's office. Clearly, there'd been quite a fight in the lab—one that had probably started out there, then ended in the office. Judging by the blood trail, Lombard had been stabbed repeatedly before dragging himself back here.

But why? To reach the phone? There were plenty of bloody fingerprints and smears around the desk, but none on the phone itself. Even though there was no evidence that he'd made a call, Hud scribbled a reminder in his notebook to pull the local usage details on Lombard's office, home and cell numbers. If nothing else, an earlier call might give them a clue as to who he'd been meeting on campus after hours.

The man must have been expecting company, judging by the two untouched shot glasses and pricey bottle of rye whiskey sitting on the coffee table in front of the leather couch. The bottle still had a red wax seal over the lid, indicating Lombard and his guest hadn't gotten around to pouring drinks. Had his killer been here to make a business deal? Was someone offering money for or demanding results from his research? Murder was one way to resolve a disagreement in terms—or to ensure a deal before those terms could be changed.

And if the victim hadn't been trying to reach the phone to call for help, then what had he been after? Why not use the cell phone linked to his name to call 911? Why not crawl to the door and shout for the guard downstairs to help him? Or trip the security alarm? The guard had indicated that opening any of these doors without the right card swipe and passcode would trigger an alarm at the security desk and at the campus security office. And why hadn't the guard responded to a brawl of this magnitude in the first place? The guy would have to be deaf not to hear the shattering glass and shifting of furniture and equipment.

Hud studied a neat, rectangular void in the blood pool. On a hunch, he pulled his own cell phone from his pocket and held it over the empty spot, confirming his suspicions before snapping a picture.

Keir appeared in the doorway, pausing to pull on his own shoe covers. "Find something?"

"Lombard's cell phone is missing, right?"

His partner crossed the room. "The ME couldn't find it anywhere on him. Just his wallet, watch and his glasses case. He had a wad of cash on him, so I think we can rule out a robbery. Although, I don't know what half that equipment out there is for. Something could be missing. We'll need to talk to someone on his staff."

Hud pointed to the open safe and file cabinet in the corner. "Those drawers don't hold anything but personnel files and student records. The safe has been ransacked, but the perp left a box of rocks behind."

"A box of rocks?"

Hud had been skeptical, too, until he opened the container and read the packing slip inside. "*Gold* rocks. The university shipped it in from Lukinburg. Over twelve thousand dollars' worth. Apparently, there's some science-y thing they do with it."

Keir let out a low whistle. "So, we're not looking at a robbery. Still, either the perp knew the combination to that safe or Lombard opened it before he was killed."

"Or he was forced to open it. Maybe the perp didn't find what he wanted and lost his temper."

"Could this be industrial espionage?"

"Possibly. We'll need to check Lombard's computer, broaden our search for missing flash drives." Hud pushed to his feet. "Check out that void. It's the same size as my phone."

"You think the killer stole Lombard's phone? Would it have a big enough memory to store his research data?"

"I'm not tech savvy enough to know. But it could hold contact information that identifies the killer, or something else incriminating, like a picture or text." Stepping across the spot where Dr. Lombard had died, Hud pointed to a second, much smaller stain several feet from where the body had been found. "What do you make of that? I'm wondering if the killer got hurt, too. That happens a lot with stabbings. We might get DNA."

Keir checked his notes. "The security guard seems to think it's from the witness."

"We have a witness?" Hud's job just got simpler if they could get a description of what had happened or who the perp might be.

Keir's weary sigh blew the idea of *simpler* out of the water. Apparently, nothing was going to come easy for Hud tonight. "One of the lab staff found Lombard before he died. Called 911 and tried to administer first aid."

"Any dying declarations from the victim?"

"Haven't talked to her yet. The paramedics are checking her out. Blow to the head. She's lucky she's not dead, too, walking into the middle of a crime like that."

*Her. She.* Apprehension knotted in his gut. "My luck with women hasn't been stellar lately. Why don't you handle the witness interviews. I'll stay up here and see if I can find whatever was used as the murder weapon."

"Unless the killer took that with him, too."

Hud nodded at the possibility, if not probability, that he wouldn't find the weapon here. If the killer had been clearheaded enough to pick up the victim's cell phone, then he wouldn't forget to take the murder weapon. "Doesn't mean I'm not going to try."

Keir pocketed his notebook. "I need to finish up with Officer Galbreath. Have him run me through the security system. A lot of it's computerized, apparently. He showed me where he reset the breaker in the basement after the power outage."

"Give me a good gun and a guard dog any day over all that high-tech mumbo jumbo," Hud grumbled. "It's too easy to hack into or override a system and cover up any sign of what's been done. I hate all those nano-bits sneaking around behind my back."

"This *is* the school of technology," Keir reminded him with a teasing grin. "Not everybody's as old-fashioned as you are, my friend."

"Have I told you to bite me lately?"

"Not for an hour or so."

Hud made an exaggerated show of typing the reminder into his phone. "I'll add looking for a way to overload the circuitry while I'm up here."

"Maybe our witness can help with that. Besides giving us a rundown on anything that might be missing." Keir backed toward the hallway. "I can talk to her as soon as I'm done with Galbreath and the medics clear her." He hesitated a moment, wanting to say something more.

"What?"

"You know I was just giving you grief at the Shamrock earlier. Don't give up on the idea of finding the right woman. Other than Dad, you're the babysitter Kenna trusts most with Lilly. And look at Millie—she's practically adopted you because she thinks you're a prize." A married woman, a baby and Keir's stepgrandmother. Yeah, Hud had a real prowess with women, so long as they were taken, under the age of two or over seventy-five. "Don't let the fact that this witness is a woman get in your head. You won't screw anything up by talking to her."

"Not tonight." Hud combed his fingers through his hair, then shook it back into its spiky disarray. His heart and his ego had taken one too many hits lately to trust that he wouldn't scare off a fragile woman with the wrong word or stupid impulse. "I'll owe you a solid if you take this interview for me."

Keir considered the bargain for a moment, then nodded. "I'll ask one of the unis to hold her until I'm done with Galbreath. He's retired KCPD, so his testimony should be reliable. But…"

*But* was not an encouraging word. "But what?"

"Galbreath claims he might have been drugged. He insists that no one could have gotten in or out of Lombard's lab and office without a key card and passcode, even with the power off. I'll ask him to report to the crime lab for a blood draw. See if there's anything in his system."

Relieved to be focusing on the case and not his own shortcomings again, Hud exhaled a measured breath. "That would explain why he didn't see or hear anything. Lombard must have known his killer if he loaned him a key card or brought him in with him. Sounds like premeditation to me if the killer knew to take out the guard, and how to get around the security system." He surveyed the trashed lab, shaking his head. "This mess looks like a disagreement that got way out of hand, though. Impulsive, not planned."

"Maybe the guard's covering for falling asleep on the job. I'll press him on it, see if I can get him to admit anything." Keir paused in the doorway and turned. "You'll be okay on your own?"

Wasn't that the irony of the evening? Hud snickered a wry laugh and waved his partner out the door. "I'll manage."

"The ME will run a full autopsy, but he says the victim probably died from exsanguination, either from the multiple wounds, or one that nicked an artery or internal organ. He suspects we're looking for something long, sharp and jagged. Probably not an actual knife." Hud had suspected as much. He was looking for a weapon of opportunity. Unfortunately, the lab had plenty of possibilities. "Should I send the CSIs up?"

Hud nodded, already spotting something he wanted to investigate. "Yeah. We'll need a team to clear this place."

Keir left to meet up with the security guard who was waiting downstairs with the uniformed officers who'd cordoned off the building. Meanwhile, Hud squatted down to snap a picture of glass shards from several beakers and a door that had shattered when a stainless steel table had tipped over into the storage cabinet where they were shelved. If there was a longer piece, it might do as a murder weapon. He'd ask the lab techs to collect the glass and piece it back together to see if a big enough sliver was missing.

He moved on to a narrow tube of steel sticking out from beneath a metal cart. A Bunsen burner. It had a long cylindrical shape with a ridged rim at the top that could account for a jagged entry wound if the killer was strong enough to drive the blunt tip through the skin. The scattered drips of blood dotting the debris that had spilled out of the cabinet and off metal trays from the table were cast-off drops, not indicators that any of these items were the actual weapon. But there were dozens of possibilities littered throughout the lab. Scissors. Giant tweezers. Even some of the knobs on this equipment could be broken off and used to stab someone.

Hud was photographing the possibilities of a good, old-fashioned toolbox that lay open on the floor inside a storage closet when he heard someone softly clearing her throat at the open doorway.

"Good. I can use the backup," he answered. "All I'm doing is taking pictures. I haven't touched anything. I'll be done with my initial scan in a few minutes." He dropped to his knees to count the number of screwdrivers in the top tray of the toolbox. "The number-one thing we need to find is the murder weapon. You can start in the office."

"Okay," a soft voice answered. He heard tentative footsteps, as if the CSI was tiptoeing around the evidence scattered across the floor.

*Okay?* No warnings about detectives disturbing potential clues and giving orders? No complaints about already having to wait for the ME and how the clock was ticking away on their Friday night plans?

Hud turned his head toward the unexpected acquiescence in that one word.

From this vantage point near the floor, all he saw were a pair of killer black high-heeled pumps. He frowned. What crime-scene technician reported for duty dressed like that? Hud sat back on his heels. "Where are your booties?"

The sexy heels stopped. "Booties?"

With a tabletop of equipment and half the lab between them, his view of the woman hadn't improved much. And yet, the scenery had improved in a way that stirred a heated interest in his blood.

Through the open space beneath the table, the high heels connected to bare legs that went up and up. He took in miles of creamy skin stretched tautly over strong calves. A sweet curve at the knee. His gaze traveled three or four inches higher until he finally ran into a hem of shimmery black material. For a man who was vertically challenged, he'd never had a problem admiring legs that were long and lean and…

There was a smear of blood on her left thigh. A circle of crimson darkened the sequins above the smear. The observation splashed cold water on the awareness sizzling through him. Blood on her skin, but no sign of a cut or scrape. Not her blood, he hoped. "Ma'am, do you have authorization to be in here?"

"The officer downstairs said the detectives wanted to talk to me."

"Ah, hell." Hud pocketed his phone and pushed to his feet. "Don't move."

His initial fascination with those sexy legs dampened with a tinge of concern and anger. This must be the witness, the woman who'd found Ian Lombard and tried to save him. Somehow, she'd missed connecting with Keir. As he rose, he finished his assessment of the woman's appearance. The cream-colored sweater she wore was stretched out of shape and spotted with more blood. The sweater was pulled tight over the flare of her hips. The front overlapped and was held in place by tightly crossed arms. The rolled-up cuffs were stained with blood, too. In her fingers, she clutched an ice pack.

His gaze finally reached a long strand of straight, brick red hair, caught in the clasp of her arms across her chest. Then he saw the swanlike neck, the gently pointed chin, the glasses over dove-gray eyes and… Any lingering lust burned completely out of his system as recognition kicked in with a vengeance. He was embarrassed that he'd ogled her like that for even one moment. That he'd equated *sexy* with any part of her.

This woman was a nerdy mix of brains and class. She was awkwardly shy, too complicated for him to fully understand and not anybody he should be getting hot and bothered over. And she had absolutely no business showing up at his crime scene covered in blood.

"What the hell?" Gigi Brennan's was not the face he was expecting to see. "What are you doing here?"

## Chapter Three

Even with the headache throbbing at her temples, Gigi recognized the square jaw dusted with golden-brown stubble and the abundant muscles that belonged to Detective Hudson Kramer. The charming remnants of the Ozark twang that colored his voice and his warm brown eyes had been the stuff of her limited fantasies for two years now. He'd been her first grown-up kiss and the last one that mattered since the fateful night when they'd first and last met.

The tiny snowflakes of light that danced through her vision, a by-product of the goose egg at the back of her head, painted the detective in a gauzy haze as he crossed the room and took her by the elbow to walk her into the hallway where the lights weren't quite as bright. Even if she didn't trust her vision, his firm grip and the scent and sound of warm, supple leather moving with every fluid step were firmly imprinted in her memories.

"Downstairs," he ordered, pulling her along beside him.

He escorted her all the way to the lobby where he halted beside Jerome's desk. He swung his gaze back and forth and muttered a curse, clearly looking for something he wasn't finding.

She scanned the lobby with him, taking in the uniformed officers and campus security on both sides of the floor-to-ceiling windows that framed the building's front doors. The ones inside were engaged with various conversations on their radios and with each other, while the officers outside were herding curious students and a growing group of reporters away from the building, ambulance and squad cars parked at the curb in front of the building.

"Did you lose someone?" she asked, her voice little more than a whisper.

But he'd heard her. "My partner."

He grumbled the words like another curse. Gigi was about to suggest she come back at a better time when a bright beam of light flashed in her eyes. Pain seared through her brain and she had to squeeze her eyes shut and turn away from the glare.

"Damn reporters. We don't even know what's going on yet, and they want the big story." Detective Kramer tightened his grip again and ushered her over to one of the small decorative trees in a giant pot in the corner of the lobby. "Sorry about that. You're the witness who found Lombard?"

"Yes." She was slightly breathless from the spike of pain through her eyes and her quick hike up and down the stairs. Or maybe slightly breathless was the way she always reacted when she thought of Hudson Kramer.

"Keir must still be downstairs with Galbreath." Detective Kramer scanned the lobby one more time before huffing a sigh and reaching inside his jacket to pull out the badge hanging from a chain around his neck. "Professor Brennan? I don't know if you remember me. I'm Detective Hudson Kramer." He held up the badge to identify himself as KCPD. "We met a while back at the Shamrock Bar. We played pool."

Gigi didn't need to see his badge, or the gun strapped to the belt of his jeans to remember the spiky brown hair and teasing smile. "I know who you are, Detective. You were interested in my sister, Tammy, that night. But she was hitting on the guy you were with, so you settled for spending the evening with me." She adjusted her glasses on the bridge of her nose, a long-ingrained habit that surfaced whenever she felt particularly self-conscious. She doubted he remembered that evening as clearly as she—few people ever obsessed over minutiae the way she did. "You were kind enough not to leave me stranded there when Tammy left with your friend. He was your partner, wasn't he?"

"Still is." That teasing smile appeared as the tension radiating from him eased. "Keir met the woman he wound up marrying that night…after he realized nothing was going to happen with your sister."

Since Tammy hadn't mentioned Keir Watson again, Gigi supposed her sister hadn't felt a spark of attraction, either. Not the way Gigi had been fascinated with this man. "Tammy said he was a gentleman. A change of pace from the men she usually dates. I'm glad things worked out for him. Sorry you didn't get a chance to hang out with her, that you got stuck with me."

"*Stuck* isn't the word I'd use. I didn't mind giving

you a ride home." Once they got to her 1940s bungalow, he'd walked her to her front door and, after a brief hesitation, had muttered something like, *What the hell*, and leaned in to give her a good-night kiss.

His fingers had tunneled into her hair to hold her mouth close to his. His stubble had tickled her lips. His heat had warmed her mouth. His touch held a faintly possessive claim she'd never experienced before. She'd barely gotten past her startled response and parted her lips to kiss him back when his hips bumped against hers and her back was against the solid oak door. His tongue speared between her lips and rolled against hers. She'd tasted the tang of beer on his tongue and felt the unyielding impression of rough denim and hard muscles pressed against nearly every part of her. Her small breasts grew heavy with the friction of his chest brushing against them. She wanted to mimic everything his mouth was doing to hers, explore the silk of his hair and the sandpapery contrast of the stubble along his jaw. But just as she was discovering every taste, every texture, every masculine scent about the man, he was pulling away. He smiled, unclutched her fingers from the warm cotton of his shirt and politely bid her good-night. Even though she'd blown that kiss, Gigi could still recall the feel of his firm, warm lips demanding something from hers. She remembered how her body had tingled and desire had rushed straight to her head like a runaway train.

Apparently, trains hadn't crashed in any memorable way for Hudson, though. He probably didn't even remember that kiss. "You turned out to be quite the pool player. I enjoyed my evening."

Not enough to follow up and call her afterward. But then, no one ever did. Gigi dipped her chin and tucked a long, loose strand of hair behind her ear. The subtle touch was another trick she used to turn the focus of her thoughts to something she was far more comfortable with than hormones and emotions. "You showed me how to play, and I'm a fast learner. Pool is basic geometry and physics. Once you figure out the angle and how much you need to spin the ball, if at all, the shots were easy."

There it was—that blank stare that indicated she'd either said something the man didn't understand, or she'd bored him into losing interest in the conversation with her logic speak.

And there was the polite smile. Nice guys always smiled before leaving. The louts just rolled their eyes and walked away, or worse, made a joke about how she didn't make sense before they went and told their friends to steer clear of Professor Brainiac.

But the usual routine ended there, leaving *her* the confused one when Detective Kramer laughed. It was a rich, robust sound from deep in his chest. "Remind me to hire you as my secret weapon the next time some dumbass challenges me to a game. I'd stop losin' money." The laughter stopped as quickly as it had started, and Hudson peered through the lenses of her glasses, making her drop her gaze. "You got a good whack on your head, didn't you? The lights bothering you in here?"

She didn't realize she'd been squinting at him until he mentioned it. "A little."

"Come on. I was going to let Keir handle the interviews. But since he's busy, let's find someplace quiet to sit down and answer a few questions." His fingers folded more gently around her elbow to pull her into step beside him again. Hud notified one of the officers to give them some privacy, then pushed the front door open for her. After briefly sizing up the crowd of onlookers and press gathering beyond the yellow crime scene tape at the end of the front walk, he steered her over to a landscaped seating area. "It's wet out here. Do you mind?"

Right now, she'd go anywhere, as long as it was away from the lights and reporters and curious faculty and students. She shook her head.

With an assortment of shrubs and the trunk of a golden-leaved pin oak between them and the crowd, he led her to a metal bench. "You look like you're dead on your feet."

"Not as dead as Dr. Lombard."

He laughed again. "You're funny, Professor. Oh…" His smile flatlined. "You weren't making a joke. Sorry."

"That would be a humorous play on words," she admitted, hearing the phrasing a moment too late. "I suppose I was pointing out the obvious."

He pulled a blue bandanna from his back pocket and wiped the lingering water droplets off the metal plank before sitting down. "It's a little cold, but we'll warm it up soon enough."

*Warm it up?* Neurons must be misfiring in her

brain. He surely didn't mean…that he would… Now? With her?

"You and Lombard were close?" he asked, patting the bench beside him.

Definitely a misfire. Gigi blinked the confusion from her panicked thoughts and sank onto the edge of the bench. The detective wanted to ask questions about Ian's murder, not exchange body heat. Maybe she *did* have a concussion that had rattled her brain.

Hudson leaned against the back of the bench, no doubt hoping his relaxed posture would encourage her to do the same.

But holding herself ramrod straight and hugging her sweater around her for warmth seemed to be the only things keeping her together tonight. She didn't think Hudson made her nervous so much as her reactions to him did. It was one thing to treasure a memory and spin a few fantasies about a man who was earthy and sexy and unlike the polished, intellectual egoists she usually spent time with. It was something else entirely to carry on a cogent conversation with the real man. Especially with her head throbbing and her emotions reeling from all she'd been through tonight.

"Ian was my boss. My mentor. A friend, too, I suppose. We made a good team. He had the ideas, and I had the patience to make them happen. I could pick up the errors in his formulas and rework the elements to complete prototypes of the technology he designed."

"He's the front man and you're the backup singer. But you need both to make the record happen."

"That analogy works. He gave me a break when some other universities wouldn't. Ian hired me to be the lead on his research team, coordinating with the visiting Lukin professor and managing the Williams U staff."

"You're kind of young for all that responsibility, aren't you?"

Gigi shrugged. She'd always been the youngest in almost every situation—school, research, learning about life. "I'm an overachiever. And I'm…smart."

"I remember that." His eyes crinkled with a smile. "When we first met you told me you'd already earned your Ph.D. That you might have earned it a year sooner if you hadn't taken several months off to take custody of your sister and handle the details of losing your parents. Reminded me of my situation growing up with my younger brother and sisters. You and I were both orphans suddenly saddled with a family to raise. Gave us something to talk about."

That was when she realized that she *was* talking to Hudson Kramer. About things other than work. Even though she'd been a dork about what drink to order and not knowing how to play pool, he'd made her feel like he understood what she meant when she rambled on or couldn't find the right words. The more time they'd spent together that night, the more she realized she wasn't completely tongue-tied with a man. She admired his commitment to his family and felt honored that he'd shared something so personal from his life. He'd made it easier for her to open up and share about hers.

Apparently, he still had a knack for getting her to open up.

"Teaching isn't really my forte. I didn't get a stellar

recommendation on my classroom performance from the school where I did my doctoral thesis. But I'm really good in the lab. Ian saw that, and he gave me the chance to work here on groundbreaking research, to get my name under his on a couple of papers we've published." Ian Lombard may have done more for her than she'd realized. "My teaching has improved with his coaching. I do better with the smaller classes here at Williams."

"You get nervous in front of a crowd?"

"I get nervous in front of anybody. But you already know that. That night at the Shamrock, you were hoping that Tammy wanted to pick *you* up. She's the social one. She's comfortable with friends or a room full of strangers." Gigi squeezed the mushy ice pack in her grip, almost surprised to find it still there. She slid a glance at Hudson, wondering if tonight was making any more sense for him than it was for her. "Did you know that research shows public speaking causes more stress for individuals than dealing with death or divorce?"

"I did not know that." Nor did he understand why she'd pointed out that fact to him—judging by the questioning arch of his right eyebrow. "Here." He plucked the ice pack from her fingers and reached behind her to find the knot in her scalp above the remnants of her bun and gently place it there. He guided her fingers up to hold it in place. "That's not doing any good in your lap." He leaned forward, bracing his elbows on his knees, possibly trying to make himself look smaller and less threatening? She might top him by an inch or two in height, but there was no way to diminish how the brown leather of his jacket stretched tautly across his broad shoulders and muscular arms and bulged over the gun strapped to his waist. His drawl might be charming, his eyes kindly indulgent, but physically, he was coiled dynamite. She was in the midst of analyzing why her pulse quickened at that metaphoric assessment when he turned his face to hers and said, "You're talking to me okay."

Startled to be caught staring at his masculine shape, Gigi snapped her gaze up to his. She looked away just as quickly, thrusting her free hand into the pocket of her sweater, curling her fingers into the thinning knots of wool—yet another trick to short-circuit her panicky thoughts and give her shy energy someplace to go. Now she could focus on the reason they were talking at all. "This conversation has a purpose. If I'm assigned a task, I will get it done. You need to know about Ian. What I saw in the lab. What I know of his timeline tonight. If I recognized the person who hit me. Details. I'm good with details."

"I'd like to know all of that if you're up to it." He pulled a notepad and pen from inside his jacket and flipped through several pages with scribbled words and a crude outline of the lab and Ian's office. "Tell me what happened tonight. Just as you remember it."

For several minutes, Hudson took notes while Gigi told him about the party and taking the bus back to campus, how she'd found Jerome asleep and thought that strange. She mentioned the suspicious power outage and how she'd discovered Ian in his office and tried to save him. Hudson continued to brace his elbows on his knees, leaning forward while she sat up straight beside him and talked to the back of his thick brown hair.

She was curious about the two lines he scratched beneath the words *Still Alive* before he asked, "Lombard told the security guard he was meeting someone here tonight. Do you know if it was a man or woman? There were two glasses set out on the table in his office."

Gigi mentally replayed the snapshots of everything that had passed by in a panicked blur earlier, stopping on the memory he wanted. "Cut-glass old-fashioned glasses. With a whiskey bottle. A brand I couldn't afford. Ian had expensive tastes."

Hudson was grinning when he turned his face to her. "You *do* notice details."

Was he making fun of her obsessive observational skills? "Isn't that what witnesses do?"

"Not necessarily." He sat up, angling his body toward hers. She jumped inside her skin when his knee brushed against hers, but quickly squelched the instinct to slide away from the warm denim. He probably hadn't even noticed the contact. And he certainly hadn't reacted as if they'd traded an electric shock the way she had. He'd think her rude. Or arrogant if he thought she was avoiding his touch. It wouldn't be the first time a man had misinterpreted her skittish reactions. "You'd be surprised how adrenaline, shock or whatever emotions they're feeling can affect how a person remembers what they've seen."

"Isn't what I'm saying accurate?" Maybe he did think something was off with her. He had to understand it was her social skills that went on the fritz around a man she was attracted to. But no one should question her intellect. "I don't usually make mistakes. Not with—"

"The details," he finished for her. He chuckled in his throat. "I trust your memory more than most, Professor. Now tell me, did Dr. Lombard leave the party early to meet somebody?"

"He didn't say anything to me. But…"

When she didn't complete the sentence, Hudson dipped his head to look up into her eyes. "But?"

Good grief. His eyes weren't just brown. They were flecked with honey and cinnamon and even a bit of mossy green. Hazel eyes. Why hadn't she noticed that before?

"Professor?"

Right. Gigi blinked away her fascination. This was not a scientific experiment on the intriguing variegations of iris color in the adult male. He was a detective and she was a witness. *Answer the question, already.* Gigi turned away slightly, breaking the innocent contact with his knee and gaze so she could focus. "Ian had an argument with one of the visiting professors, Evgeni Zajac from the University of Saint Feodor in Lukinburg. I don't know what it was about, other than Dr. Zajac accused Ian of something. Evgeni doesn't speak very good English, so I'm surprised it lasted as long as it did. I don't know where his translator, his wife Hana Nowak, was." She rubbed her fingers over the bruises Evgeni had left on her upper arms. "Evgeni thought Ian was hiding from him. Maybe their argument upset him, and that's why Ian forgot me."

"Forgot you?"

He asked her to spell Professor Zajac's name before she answered. "Ian gave me a ride to the reception. That's how he convinced me to go."

"By promising you wouldn't be alone with all those people."

Gigi nodded.

"And then he left without you. Hence, the bus." The dark eyebrow arched again. "Even I've had better dates. And that's saying something."

"It wasn't a date." She hastened to correct the detective's misconception of her relationship with her boss. "I wasn't his type."

The evocative eyebrow flattened with a frown. "Lombard had a type?"

With the ice pack mostly melted and her arm tiring from holding it in place, Gigi set it on the bench beside her and buried her cold fingers in the pocket of her sweater, flexing them around the cell phone she carried there. She felt guilty for even thinking ill of the dead. Although he'd never been anything but kind and supportive to her, Ian Lombard had had two major shortcomings—an ego that matched his IQ and a weakness for a pretty face.

But then Hudson touched his pen to the back of her knuckles through the knitted wool, stilling the outward manifestation of her internal debate. The touch startled her into looking into those eyes again. "Cold?" he asked. "Do we need to go back inside?"

She shook her head, wondering if he'd picked up on the way she touched her glasses or clothes or hair to break into her thoughts when she got stuck inside her head. "It's a habit. It calms me. I hate clothes that don't have any pockets."

"Me, too." With the barest hint of a smile crinkling the corners of his eyes, he said, "Tell me about Lombard's type, and how a leggy redhead like you doesn't qualify."

*Leggy redhead?* Was that a compliment? No. She tamped down that rush of anticipation that surged through her. It was a statement of fact. She did have long legs and auburn hair. But it was sweet that he'd noticed a couple of *details* about her, too. Hudson Kramer really was surprisingly easy to talk to.

"Dr. Lombard used to..." Was there any polite way to say this? "He's—was—a married man. But he had wandering eyes. He flirted with some of the students. They'd meet for...consultations...in his office. Sometimes, after hours."

"He liked them young."

"And blonde. And curvy. He even asked me about Tammy after she stopped by to take me to lunch on my birthday last year." That had been the first time she'd explained the ground rules of sexual harassment to Ian, and why their students and her sister were off-limits to him.

"That could make some enemies. Did it ever go beyond flirting?"

"I couldn't say for sure," she confessed. "It never happened with me. He said he valued me too much as his assistant." It had been one of those rare times when she'd been glad she was a shy, forgettable woman who didn't turn heads. "He's been reprimanded by the university. Threatened with a sexual harassment suit. I thought he'd stopped his philandering, though. I haven't heard any recent complaints from any of my students, or gossip from the faculty and staff."

"A guy who's a player is always going to be a player. But you don't know anyone who'd carry a grudge against him for that? An angry parent? Husband? Boyfriend? The victims themselves?"

Gigi shook her head. "His wife had threatened to divorce him. But they were going through marriage counseling. She's out of the country, anyway, so it couldn't have been her."

Detective Kramer grunted as if that didn't necessarily give the woman an alibi. "What's his wife's name?"

"Doris Lombard. She's a theater arts professor here. She's on sabbatical in Norway this semester."

"Let's say Zajac didn't follow your boss here to finish the argument, and there aren't any disgruntled students who'd take exception to being pawed by a man with authority over them like that." He flipped to a new page in his notebook. "Do you know if he was having problems with anyone else?"

"Like what?"

"Anything. Personal? Professional?"

She couldn't think of any specifics, but she knew Ian hadn't been universally liked. "There's always competition in the academic world—for grant money, tenured positions, funding for programs. There are a lot of egos, too, that come into play when you're talking about that kind of money."

"What kind of money are we talking about?"

Gigi considered some of the numbers Ian had

bragged about—numbers that seemed to have made his wife overlook those dalliances with younger women. "Thousands. Millions. Not just for the university, but for whoever holds the patents for various discoveries. Sometimes companies or alumni investors will pay a stipend for research or teaching programs above and beyond university funding."

"Did anybody think Lombard had stolen their patent? Or taken credit for research that wasn't his?"

Mentally running through a list of jealous coworkers and competitors, Gigi almost missed the squishing of dead leaves and wet mulch behind her. Before she could turn to see who was approaching, Hudson sprang to his feet. "Stop right there." He pulled back the front of his jacket, exposing his badge and resting his hand on the butt of his gun. "This is a crime scene and you're trespassing."

Gigi rose to her feet, recognizing the stink of too much cologne.

This was *not* what she needed tonight.

## Chapter Four

"Gigi? Darling, I just heard. You poor thing." *Darling?* The tall man with wire-rimmed glasses and a neatly trimmed blond beard rushed up to Gigi and pulled her into his chest, hugging his arms around her. "I can't believe someone killed Ian. What is this world coming to?"

"Gary." Water dripped from his hair and ran down her neck as her cheek smushed against the scratchy tweed of his jacket. "I don't need a hug right now."

"I always said you needed to be running that program. You or me." Ignoring her protest, he shook his head spraying her with more droplets. "Ian was a front man—you were the workhorse who covered his ass more than once."

"Gary!"

She'd gotten one hand free to palm against his tweed lapel when a second, stronger hand did something to Gary's grip and pried her free.

Gigi stepped back to brush the moisture from her skin while Hudson's shoulder moved into the space between them. He flashed his badge. "Detective Hudson Kramer, KCPD. We're having a conversation here. Police business."

"Police?" Rubbing his wrist and looking confused, Gary glanced from the badge to Hud and over to Gigi. "Were you here when Ian was killed? Do you need me to call an attorney for you?"

"No—"

"They don't suspect you had anything to do with this, do they?"

"I don't think they—"

"We don't," Hudson stated emphatically. "She's a witness, not a suspect. I'm going to have to ask you to leave right now, sir."

"What happened?" Gary asked, deaf to both Detective Kramer's request and Gigi's distress.

The image of puncture wounds and shredded clothes and skin was branded on Gigi's brain. "He was stabbed. Several times."

"How awful." Gary's blue-eyed gaze darted down to her sweater as she rolled the stained cuffs back into place. "Oh, my God. Are you hurt?"

He stepped around Hud.

"It's not my blood."

His arms stretched out toward her.

She tried to retreat, but her legs hit the bench. "Don't—"

A wall of brown leather filled her vision as Hud once again inserted himself between Gigi and the man she'd spent far too many hours with in the lab. "Okay, pal. Next time I won't ask nicely. She said to back off."

"I work here. We're friends," Gary insisted, briefly

tilting his gaze down to Hudson. "More than friends. Tell him, darling."

The endearment made her skin crawl. "Stop calling me that."

"We've gone out several times—"

"Once."

"What's your name, sir?" Hud asked.

"And whose fault is that?"

"Name."

The tall man's gaze darted back and forth, as if he didn't quite understand why Hud kept interrupting him. "Gary Haack. *Professor* Gary Haack." He emphasized the title, just like he'd emphasized his family's money and all the things that made him a good catch on that *one date* when he'd taken her to dinner and the symphony. "I'm with the engineering department. I head up Lombard's research team. Along with Gigi," he added, either as an afterthought or a reason to explain his claim on her. "Tell him, darling."

"ID."

Gary's eyes landed squarely on Hudson now. He lifted his chin to an arrogant tilt. "I am not some common criminal. I'm here to support Miss Brennan."

"*Professor* Brennan," Hud corrected. "And she's not your darlin'." Gigi felt something warm inside her at the subtle defense of her honor and hard work. She'd gotten used to fending off Gary's attention all by herself. She'd gotten used to doing a lot of things on her own. Was it any wonder that she'd fashioned Hudson Kramer into some kind of champion after one evening of playing pool at a bar and one awkward yet memorable kiss? He was still waiting, still not giving a flying flip about Gary's claim that he had a right to be here. "ID."

Grumbling a protest, Gary pulled out his wallet and handed Hud his driver's license. "Here. But if you won't let me comfort her, you must at least let me do my job." Hud jotted down the information while somehow keeping a sharp eye on Gary who leaned to the side to address Gigi directly. "We need to get ahead of this and do damage control. Do the investors know yet? They know we can continue Ian's work without him, right?"

The investors were the last thing on her mind right now. Gigi hugged her arms in front of her, jarred by the abrupt change in topic. "I don't know. There are reporters here, but I don't think they've broadcast anything yet. Why aren't you still at the reception? And why is your hair wet, but not your clothes?" It had always been easier to analyze details than to process emotions for her.

"Reporters, right." Ignoring every question, Gary adjusted his glasses and smoothed his damp hair into place. "I'll make a statement to them. Represent the department since I'm sure you're not up for that. As for the reception, except for Ambassador Poveda, once Ian disappeared, Dr. Zajac and the rest of the Lukin representatives left." Gary paused with his hand on the knot of his tie. "Speaking of… Here comes Zajac now."

Sure enough, she spotted Evgeni Zajac's white hair, psychedelically tinted by the red-and-blue lights spinning on top of a police car parked at the curb. With his beautiful younger wife beside him, patiently translating whatever he was saying to the officer beside the police car, he gestured wildly, pointing to the building, then pointing to the crowd gathered behind the yellow crime scene tape, finally pointing to her. Once his dark eyes had zeroed in on her, he started walking toward them. He might be restricted from going inside the technology building, but there was nothing to stop him from crossing the lawn and speaking to her outside. "Gary! Gigi!"

Gigi closed her eyes against the dizzying discomfort that swept through her at the idea of facing more people. With the ground spinning beneath her feet, she grabbed on to the most solid thing she could find and ended up clutching a handful of soft, worn leather. When her fingertips dug into the muscle of Hudson Kramer's arm, she felt a warm hand covering hers. "You okay?"

She opened her eyes at the husky drawl to discover Hudson's golden eyes looking into hers. Before she could process the concern in those eyes, before she could explain the tightness in her stomach or even say she wasn't feeling well, Evgeni and his wife, Hana Nowak, joined them.

Dr. Zajac was the first to speak. "Can we get into the lab? Is our work safe?" He made no mention of, much less apologized for, the way he'd treated her at the reception. "Was any of our classified work taken or destroyed? The gold?"

"We don't know that yet," Gary answered. "Gigi was a witness—"

"A witness?" Hana Nowak's dark eyes, filled with pity, turned to her. Her accent was far less pronounced than her husband's. "You were there when Ian died?"

"—but I haven't been able to get two words in edgewise with her," Gary continued.

Evgeni demanded a translation from his wife.

"Hey!" Hud's voice topped them all. Gary, Hana and Dr. Zajac all snapped their attention to him. "This isn't a party. You all need to leave."

Hana was the first one to accede. "Of course. You have work to do." She tugged on her husband's arm. "Ev. Can't you see Gigi is in mourning? This is the time for sympathy, not work. I am so sorry, my dear." Hana leaned over the back of the bench to pull Gigi in for a hug. Although the position was awkward, the other woman's grief seemed genuine. Gigi wound her arms lightly around her and held on long enough to hear the sniffle of tears against her collarbone. "I know Ian was your dear friend. He was a great man. I am sorry for you," she added, blinking back tears as she pulled away. She reached into her husband's pocket for a handkerchief and dabbed at her nose.

"Thank you, Hana." The thirtysomething woman's black hair hung in a smooth, damp ponytail down her back. She must have been caught out in the rainstorm, too. Only, her wet hair looked sleek and shiny, like thin strands of polished obsidian, while Gigi's bun was a mess and her loose hair was frizzing with the humidity lingering in the air.

Hana linked her arm through her much older husband's. "Evgeni expresses his condolences, as well."

When she turned a reproving gaze up at him, he shrugged. "Of course. It is a great tragedy to lose a mind like Ian's." He turned to his wife and asked her something in Lukin.

Hana's eyes widened before she repeated it in English. "Has anyone notified Doris Lombard yet? Evgeni believes his wife should be the one handling the arrangements for Ian's funeral, and give permission before there is any kind of autopsy."

"A crime has been committed, ma'am," Hud explained. "Mrs. Lombard doesn't get to say whether there's an autopsy or not. The ME will handle it. And yes, Mrs. Lombard has been notified by the police. She's been informed of the suspicious circumstances and is making arrangements to get back to Kansas City."

"Poor Doris," Hana offered. Evgeni muttered something about Ian's shortcomings as a husband, and Hana yanked on his arm, her cheeks coloring with embarrassment. "It is not wise to speak ill of the dead." She apologized to the rest of them for whatever her husband continued to grumble about. "I am so sorry."

"You had no love for Ian Lombard?" Hud asked, finally returning Gary's license.

"None of us did," Gary answered. Dr. Zajac nodded his agreement. "Ian was a brilliant man, but he could be a jerk to work with." He pointed to Gigi. "Ask her. She cleaned up after him more than he deserved."

"Please don't say anything...like that...to the reporters," Gigi pleaded. "Ian was temperamental, but he was always good to me—like a father figure."

He rolled his eyes up to the stars with an impatient huff. "You were his prized possession. The academic whiz kid he discovered who made him look better

than he was." Although his tone was filled with concern, Gary's choice of words made her uneasy. "Is
that what you want me to tell the reporters? That you
two were close?"

"I don't want you to mention me at all. And I don't
want you to smear Ian's reputation. That would be a
blot on the university. On the program. On all of us."

Evgeni muttered a phrase, which she'd learned was
a Lukin curse.

"Ev!" Hana chided. "What Gigi is saying makes
sense. We shouldn't be talking about Ian's indiscre-
tions when we are on the verge of expanding your
project's funding."

"*Our* project," Gary corrected. "We just lost one
egomaniac. I don't intend to let another take his place."

"Nobody's saying anything to any reporter until
KCPD releases an official statement." Hud put an end
to the conversation. "I need to finish interviewing Professor Brennan. Without any of you upsetting her." He
pointed to the uniformed brunette standing just inside
the main doors. "Y'all are going over to that officer
and give her your names. Then you can wait inside
the lobby. Since you knew the victim, my partner and
I will want to ask you a few questions."

Evgeni cursed at the directive. "I will do no such
thing. I did not leave my country to come here and
be treated as a criminal. I will invoke diplomatic im-
munity."

"That's your call, sir. But I'm still gonna have to
ask you to leave the crime scene."

Hana apologized for her husband's outburst and
pulled him away from the bench. "Of course, De-

tective." The couple turned toward the parking lot. "Come, *dorogoy*. We will drive to the Lukinburg Embassy and inform them of what has happened. They will want to know about the tragedy of tonight's honored guest."

Just as the overwhelming tension in the air started to dissipate, Gary stepped closer, straightening to his full height, no doubt to assert his influence and take control of the conversation. "I'm not leaving Gigi." Ignoring Hud's instruction, Gary circled around the shorter man and reached for her. "She doesn't handle interpersonal—"

"Gary, don't."

"Now—" Hud stiff-armed Gary out of her personal space "—would be a good time to go."

"She needs me." When Gary reached for her again, Hud grabbed his outstretched fingers and spun him around, twisting his arm up behind his back.

"Final warning. Next time I arrest you for interfering with a police investigation."

Gary yelped in protest but didn't struggle. "I'll have your badge for this."

"Go ahead," Hud dared him. "Report me."

Gary looked down over the jut of his shoulder at Hud. He was half a foot taller than the detective who had him pinned, but Gigi had no doubt who would win if this escalated into a physical fight. And while the realization that Hud was defending her wishes warmed her with an unfamiliar thrill, there'd already been too much violence tonight. "Please do as he says."

After shooting her a look of hurt, Gary put up his free hand in surrender. "Very well. For you." Once

Hud had released him, Gary straightened his jacket and rubbed his shoulder. "In case you didn't recognize it, I was trying to help you. I would think a familiar face would be welcome right about now." He shot an accusing glance at Hud. "You know she's not comfortable around a lot of people, right?"

"You included, apparently."

"How dare you." Gary's voice took on a harsh tone. "I am a respected member of this faculty—"

Hudson pulled out his handcuffs.

Gary held his ground. "I want to hear it from Gigi. I'm not abandoning her."

"Go," Gigi pleaded. Her nerves were frayed to the point that she couldn't hold Gary's probing gaze. "Please."

Hud's shoulders expanded with a deep, measured breath. "That means you're out of here."

Gary answered with a self-righteous snort. "I guess I'll go talk to that officer."

"I guess you will."

Seeming to understand that Hudson's words were an order, not a request, Gary headed the opposite direction in which Hana and Evgeni had disappeared. As he moved past Gigi, he held his thumb and pinkie up to his face and mouthed the words, "Call me."

Never. She would deal with all this by herself before she would agree to whatever obsessive strings Gary wanted to tie to her in exchange for his comfort and support.

"Interesting friends you've got there." After dismissing her coworkers from the conversation, Hud turned halfway to face her, and she discovered she still held a tight-fisted grip on the sleeve of his jacket. "You okay?"

As confused by the emotions clouding her thoughts as she was embarrassed at the liberty she'd taken by sinking her grip into him more than once, she released Hud's arm and the back of his jacket and collapsed onto the bench.

"Sorry," she apologized automatically. "I guess I kind of blanked out there for a few seconds. I didn't wrinkle your jacket, did I?"

"Impossible. This leather is as tough as I am." He replaced his cuffs in his pocket and sat on the bench beside her. "You didn't answer my question."

"Uh, huh." Aware that Hud had spoken, though not really hearing his response, she craned her neck over her shoulder, wondering what Gary was saying to the police officer inside the lobby, and why he had positioned himself so that he was facing Gigi through the window. Was that piercing blue gaze showing concern? Or some kind of creepy claim on her allegiance?

It must be after midnight by now. The temperature was dropping. She couldn't seem to hug herself tightly enough to stop shivering.

And then she felt the tip of a warm, calloused finger on the point of her chin. Hudson turned her face and focus back to him. "Eyes right here, G. They're not going to bother you anymore tonight."

He stroked his thumb beneath her chin, turning a very practical touch into something that felt like a caress. The tightness in her chest eased, and the cloudy air of malaise that had taken over her thoughts drifted away. She processed the husky timbre of his voice, and the odd choice of words that had pulled her back from her panicked reaction to that confrontation with Gary and the Zajacs. "G?"

He chuckled as he pulled his hand away. "It's half of Gigi. I'm lazy."

"Gigi is already short for my given name, Virginia."

"Then I'm really lazy."

The tension in her relaxed at his self-deprecating humor. "That's a goofy thing to say."

"Goofy enough to make you smile. I like this look better."

"Better than what?"

"Like you're scared of something." He glanced over at the front doors. "Or someone."

"Gary?" She slipped her coworker a glance, but he turned his back to her as soon as he realized he'd snagged Hud's attention, too. "I'm not afraid of him." She idly rubbed her arm where Evgeni had bruised her earlier. "Of any of them. I see them every day at work. I...trust them."

Even as the words left her mouth, she was revising her opinion. She'd trusted them all before tonight. Something had changed leading up to Ian's death. Egos. Secrets. Tempers. Money. Something she didn't yet understand.

Hudson looked as skeptical as she felt. "You didn't want Haack touching you. Intimating that you were more than friends. Or mentioning you to the press."

Gigi wasn't sure how to explain why she didn't want a handsome, accomplished man like Gary paying attention to her. She had next to no experience with men, but she'd like to think she could enjoy herself more with a man than the stilted conversations and end-of-the-night gropefest she'd endured on their date. "I don't mind working with him. He's good at his job. The students love him. He represents the engineering part of our technology development while I'm in charge of the physics. As the coassistant on Dr. Lombard's research project, there'd be no impropriety if I wanted to date him. We went out once. He's asked me out several times since, but…"

"But?"

"I don't want to."

"You don't want to go out with Haack?"

"I missed my whole teenage learning-about-boys-and-sex years because I was steamrolling my way through school at an accelerated rate. Then I was taking care of Tammy and now I work. I should be flattered that a man with Gary's reputation wants to have a relationship with me. But I can't tell if he really cares about me, or if I'm just the type of woman he thinks he *should* care about. I don't feel any chemistry. If I have to settle for that kind of spark-free relationship, then I will proudly wear my virgin hat until the day I die."

He laughed out loud at her answer. "Virginia Brennan, you are a unique woman. You tell it like it is, don't you."

Gigi had never thought about the sound of a man's laugh. But she liked the sound of Hudson Kramer's. It was musical, came from deep in his chest and was as genuine and easy to like as the man himself. The sound of it made her prickle with a magnetic energy, just as the tingling sensation where he'd caressed her skin earlier had. And how could his eyes pull off this gentle puppy-dog look and still have that sharp, wolf-like directness that had chased Gary and the Zajacs away?

Oh, hell. This was no fantasy. She was attracted to the real man.

"G?"

Once she realized that he'd stopped laughing, she adjusted her glasses to mask the fact that she was staring. Assessing. Appreciating. Embarrassing herself with this silly crush. And had she just admitted she'd never slept with a man? Hudson's eyes were of no consequence to her. His laughter didn't mean he thought she was funny—he was simply making her feel comfortable enough with him so she could answer his questions. He probably had a hot date waiting for him once this interview was done. She reminded herself that there was nothing personally protective about dismissing Dr. Zajac and his wife or getting Gary Haack to leave her alone. It was pure practicality. Detective Kramer had a murder to investigate, and he didn't need any interruptions when he was interrogating a witness.

"I'm sorry. That knock on the head seems to be affecting my concentration. Normally, I'm not so easily distracted." That statement was true. Although, she typically didn't spend much time in the company of a man she found so…distracting. "Did you have more questions you wanted to ask?"

A frown tightened his mouth, as if he didn't like her response. "Just one. Did you see who hit you?"

"I would have told you right away if I'd seen the killer."

"I didn't ask about Lombard's killer."

"Isn't it the same person?"

"Not necessarily. Lombard was already dying when you found him. But you experienced your attack first-hand. Your perception will be different." Okay, so not everything about Hudson Kramer was charming. Or sexy. Or distracting. That biting tone was nothing but irritated detective. "What do you remember before you were knocked unconscious? You're the expert on details. Sounds? Smells? Anything you can think of might be a clue."

Gigi closed her eyes and dutifully replayed the blurry images from her memory, looking everywhere except at the dead man beneath her hands. There'd been a glimpse of movement in the corner of her vision. "Black."

"He was a black man?"

"No. I don't know. I never saw a face. I was down on the floor with Ian. I never had a chance to look up." The sounds of Ian's labored breathing and her own frantic gasps gave way to charging footsteps. "I heard the crunch of glass first."

"There was a lot of broken glass at the crime scene. Your attacker probably couldn't avoid walking over it. And then?"

"Then I saw black. Rushing at me. Closing in all around me, it seemed. Just an impression before pain exploded in the back of my skull. Black shoes? Pants? A shadow?" She shook her head, knowing the vague description wasn't much help. "My glasses flew off and I must have passed out. Nothing was clear."

"Did you smell anything?"

Something pungent. Woodsy. Chemical? Cologne? Gigi's eyes popped open. "Alcohol."

"Medicinal? Something from the lab or cleaning crew?"

Gigi shook her head. "The kind you drink."

"There was a whiskey bottle in Lombard's office. But it was full, unopened."

"But I can still smell it." She raised the rolled-up cuff of her sweater to her nose and breathed in. "It's on me. It's in the blood that's on me."

"The murder weapon had a sharp, cylindrical shape." He wrote something in his notes and circled it three times.

"Like the neck of a broken whiskey bottle. Someone must have replaced the bottle and taken the broken one with him."

Hudson grinned, creating a flash of white in the middle of his stubbled face. "You *are* good at details."

He tucked his notebook and pen inside his jacket. The interview must be over.

"Was I helpful?"

"You did great, G." He held his hand out to her, forcing Gigi to unlock her crossed arms to take it. His grip was warm. Firm. Gentle. He released her the moment she stood. "I think you've answered enough questions for one night. We're done. Unless you think of something else that might help, or you remember any dying declarations Lombard might have said."

"Like *So-and-so killed me*?"

He grinned. "I've never been that lucky. You got someone to drive you home?" He tilted his head toward the building, indicating that Gary was watching them again. "Besides Mr. I-Got-No-Clue-About-Personal-Boundaries over there? Or Dr. Foreign Fury and his put-upon wife?"

She shook her head, unable to hide her smile at his spot-on descriptions. "I'm the one others call for that sort of thing. Designated driver for girls' night out. Getting stranded on the road. I'm usually available and willing to help."

"Watching someone who was an important part of your life die is a lot harder to deal with than helping a friend who has a flat tire. If it hasn't hit you yet, it will." She stiffened at the unexpected touch of his hand at the small of her back as he turned her toward the sidewalk. "What about your sister?"

"She's out of town. I'll be fine, Hudson..." She stopped and faced him, needing to break even that polite, impersonal contact in order to remind herself that there was nothing happening between them here, at least not on his part. "I mean Detective Kramer."

"Hudson or Hud is fine." She didn't understand how he could be friendly one moment and frowning at her the next. "You have a head injury. I'll borrow my partner's Camaro and drive you home."

So she could relive that awkward good-night kiss from two years earlier? No thanks. "The paramedic cleared me. The bleeding stopped and I don't need stitches. My pupils reacted the way they're supposed to. She told me to watch for signs of a concussion. I'm to go to the ER right away if I feel dizzy and nauseous or my headache and vision get worse."

"None of that sounds good. Let me get Keir's keys."

"That isn't necessary." This time she reached for him when he started for the building. For a split second she wondered if holding on to the man himself would be as addictive as snatching up a handful of worn leather. "My car is here. My things are in my backpack in the lobby. One of the officers wanted to look through it before removing it from the crime scene. My keys are there. As soon as I get it back, I can drive myself. I'll be fine."

"You'd better be." He winked, and a blanket of warmth fell over her at the friendly gesture and teasing tone. Fantasy or not, Hudson Kramer really was a nice guy. How could she not smile when he was so kind to her? "Let me run in and get your bag."

She was still smiling when he returned, looping the strap of her backpack over her shoulder. "Professor Haack lawyered up the moment my partner started asking questions, so we had to let him go. He said he'd come down to the precinct office tomorrow to give us an interview. In the meantime, if he gives you any more trouble over this, you give me a call, okay?"

Tempting as it might be to let Hud form a line of defense between her and the unpleasantries of her world, Gigi knew she had to rely on her own strength. She unhooked her keys and lifted her hand in a slight wave as she backed toward the parking lot. "Thank you. For everything tonight. Please catch whoever did this to Ian."

"I will."

She hesitated when he fell into step beside her. "I said you didn't need to—"

"Don't finish that sentence. You're not walking to your car by yourself at night. Especially with all you've been through."

Perhaps thinking she'd argue further, his hand settled at the small of her back, guiding her toward the parking lot. Although she didn't want to make anything too personal of his chivalry, Gigi was nonetheless relieved to have the safe escort to her car. After all, there was a murderer loose on campus, and he might just think she'd seen something incriminating. Or, without KCPD around to run interference, Gary or Dr. Zajac might chase after her for a private conversation. Plus, Hud was right. Eventually, the grief of watching her mentor die in such a violent fashion was going to catch up to her. And there really was a calming sense of protection in Hud's armed, muscular presence beside her. No one could blame her if she shortened her stride just a fraction to lean into the sheltering warmth of his touch.

Once they reached her car, Hud pulled away to hold the door while she climbed in behind the wheel. "I'll call you tomorrow to make sure you're okay. My partner and I will probably have some follow-up questions for you then. You might remember something important after the shock wears off and you've had a chance to rest up."

That sense of someone giving a damn about her well-being faded. Hudson Kramer was a kind man, yes, but he was more worried about solving Ian's murder than he was learning there was no one in her life to take care of her. She started the engine and reached for the door handle. "Good night, Detective."

He moved into the vee between the door and frame of the car and leaned in. "I thought we were going with Hud."

Suddenly, the late hour and roller-coaster ride of emotions she'd been on this evening hit her. Tears stung her eyes and she reached up beneath her glasses to wipe them away. She wasn't lying when she explained away her stilted good-night. "I think I've handled all the stress I can tonight. I'm really tired. I just want to go home."

He studied her for a moment before he straightened away from the door. "Okay, G." He closed it while Gigi started the engine. "Works for me."

Her innate curiosity about his reaction, and confusion with clever, slangy banter forced her to roll down the window. "What works for you?"

He grinned, as if her question amused him. "You going straight home and getting some rest sounds like a smart plan to me."

"What I said works for you because you approve of my plan?"

"I guess." He shrugged. "It's just a thing I say. A way to agree with someone and let 'em know I like what they said. It was good to see you again. I wish it had been under better circumstances."

"Me, too."

He stepped back as she shifted the car into Reverse. "Good night, G."

"Good night, Hud."

Gigi backed out and turned her car toward the exit.

She studied him in the rearview mirror until he turned away and headed back into the building to continue his investigation.

Hudson Kramer was physical and outgoing, while she was intellectual and too introverted for her own good. There was absolutely no spot on their personality vertices where their $x$ and $y$ axes intersected. Yet despite their differences, he'd been kind to her. He was patient with her awkwardness and didn't make her feel like five feet nine inches of weird, gawky misfit the way most men did. Who was she kidding? She made herself feel that way. Counseling in high school, assertiveness training during her graduate coursework and repeated social advice from Ian and her younger sister hadn't done much to make her comfortable in her own skin. They'd only given her strategies to cope with her shyness and social anxiety.

Work made her feel comfortable. Losing herself in the puzzle of an ongoing project. She could manage the day-to-day basics of raising her sister and earning her degrees and holding down a job. She ran her research team efficiently and earned a healthy salary that allowed her to not only buy a home in a nice neighborhood but remodel it to suit her own tastes. One-on-one, she could talk with the most influential of people when it came to her science. But social interactions? Parties? Men she was attracted to? Forget about kisses no one else remembered. She might as well dress in camouflage and disappear behind a potted plant.

## Chapter Five

Gigi's trip home took her ten minutes longer than usual because of the perennial road construction in the city narrowing busy streets to a single lane or requiring a detour. And when she'd turned off Rockhill Road to drive over to Main, she'd been certain that someone was following her. For a few brief moments she'd felt a happy warmth and then a pang of guilt, thinking Hudson Kramer was making sure she got safely home.

But then she remembered he'd said something about borrowing his partner's Camaro to drive her home, and this vehicle had too high a profile to be any kind of muscle car. Not that she was an expert on cars, but she'd guess that was an SUV or extended-cab pickup truck looming in her rearview mirror. Her grip on the steering wheel tightened with every turn the dark vehicle made with her, even speeding up to get through a yellow light behind her.

But when she turned into the historic bungalow area north of the Nelson-Atkins Museum of Art, the vehicle drove on past. She exhaled a breath she didn't realize she'd been holding and felt the last dregs of her energy waning along with her paranoia.

Driving almost by rote now, she followed the curve around Gillham Park to the row of craftsman-style bungalows where she lived. Seeing the cars parked along the curb on either side of the street was nothing new, since the houses were close together, and driveways were a relatively new update that only a few homes, like her own, had. The street meant home and the sanctuary that called to her as stress, anxiety and grief robbed her of energy and left her with a bone-numbing fatigue.

She kept having to restart the mental checklist of everything she'd need to do in the upcoming days. Take inventory of the lab and Ian's office—had anything been stolen? Was there equipment that needed to be replaced or repaired? Gary Haack had been right about one thing—the Lukin investors would need to be notified. But first she would bring her team together tomorrow, to fill them in on Ian's death. She'd need to fill out and sign a police report, so that meant a trip downtown. She'd have to set up a meeting with the dean to talk about continuing Ian's research. Did she include Dr. Zajac in that meeting? Gary? Who was responsible for cleaning up the mess in the lab? And what else could she remember that would help Hud and his partner find Ian's killer? There had to be something more useful than the smell of whiskey and a swirl of black—

"What the...?" She stomped on the brake and jerked to a halt as a black SUV swung out of her driveway, nearly clipping the front fender of her car. She honked her horn, but the warning sound was drowned out by the spinning of tires screaming to find traction on the pavement. For a split second, she relived the attack at the lab as the black vehicle lurched forward and barreled toward her. Before she could do more than glimpse the shadowy form of the driver through the windshield, the SUV ripped off her side-view mirror, scraped across the driver's-side doors and raced on to the next intersection, tires squealing around the corner before the SUV even switched on its headlights. "Stop! You... Idiot!"

Gigi's heart pounded against her rib cage, her breaths coming in shallow, panicked gasps. Her thoughts instantly went back to the vehicle that had followed her through downtown. But that had been a mistake, right? That vehicle had driven on. It couldn't have doubled back someplace and beaten her home. Could it?

Where had that SUV come from? With all the vehicles parked along the curb, she hadn't seen it backing out. Had she dozed off behind the wheel? Gotten too caught up in her thoughts to notice someone turning around in her driveway? She did have one of the few homes on the block with a driveway, so that explanation made sense. Still, the timing of the accident was unsettling. And the driver hadn't stopped, so she certainly wasn't getting anyone else's insurance to pay for her busted mirror.

For about two seconds, she considered turning around and following the SUV to at least get a license plate. But the roar of its engine faded into the night, and she doubted she'd be able to catch up to him.

Instead, she rubbed at the sore spot on her chest where the seat belt had yanked her back against the seat, and forced herself to take a deep breath, vowing to check every door and window of the house and garage to make sure she hadn't had a break-in. With her senses reawakened like a jolt from a crash cart, she eased up on the brake and pulled into her driveway.

Her headlights flashed across the back of Tammy's yellow Volkswagen. Could that be an explanation for the car that had hit hers? Gigi had driven Tammy to the airport on Wednesday. But with her car still parked here, could one of the men she dated have thought her sister was at home for a late-night rendezvous? But what man wouldn't call or text first? Someone drunk? Obsessive? Someone she probably didn't want her sister dating. Gigi found herself wishing she *had* interrupted an impromptu booty call, and that her sister was home. She could use a friendly face tonight. And a hug.

Gigi pulled up behind the VW, then unlocked her white-knuckle grip around the steering wheel and opened the door. She lifted the mirror that was dangling from a few wires and shook her head at the missing paint and dented metal. Although she was an expert in several technologies, car repairs were not in her wheelhouse. She'd have to add a visit to her insurance man and the service department at the car dealership to her list of things to get done.

"Virginia? Is that you?" The light went on at the porch next door and a feathery voice called to her across the yard. Gigi looked over the roof of her car to see her next-door neighbor Kelly Allan step outside in her chenille bathrobe. The older woman cradled her Pomeranian in her arms and hastened down the front steps as quickly as her arthritic knees would allow. "My goodness. Are you all right? I saw everything if you need a witness. You're lucky that car didn't kill you. I'm just glad Izzy had already finished her outing." She looked to the intersection where the dark vehicle had disappeared. "It's not safe for man or beast in this neighborhood, anymore."

Wisps of the woman's gray hair caught the light from her porch and framed her head like a silvery halo. But Gigi suspected there was nothing angelic or chance about this late-night meeting. Miss Allan set her tiny puff of a dog on the grass and crossed the yard while Gigi locked her car and dutifully circled around it to greet her elderly neighbor. "I hope the noise didn't frighten you. I didn't see him until he was right on me. He should have had his lights on. Of course, it's after midnight. The driver probably wasn't expecting any traffic. I'm sure we're fine now," she reassured the frail woman. "What are you doing up so late?"

Her neighbor tugged on the leash she held in her hand. "Potty training the new puppy. When Izzy says she has to go, we go."

Gigi eyed the pampered Pomeranian who hadn't been a puppy for a couple of years now. She was pawing through the red leaves that had fallen from her neighbor's dogwood tree, no doubt on the trail of a squirrel or other small rodent. Knowing Miss Allan's eccentricities, the late-night walk in her lavender robe had more to do with her hobby of spying on the neighbors than it did with walking her dog. "You probably shouldn't be outside alone at this time of night."

"You're telling me. This used to be a nice neighborhood when my parents built this house." She fluttered her manicured fingers in the air. "Now we've got strange cars parking here in the middle of the night. Or driving slowly around the block, like they're checking our houses to see which one would be easiest to break in to and rob." She softened her shrill voice to a whisper. "I thought he must be one of Tammy's young beaux, sneaking out of the house before you got home. I realize she's a grown-up now, but it still must be awkward to have your big sister interrupt when you're entertaining a young gentleman."

"Tammy's out of town, Miss Allan." That vague sense of alarm that had gone dormant since her interview with Hud resurrected itself. She glanced back at her own well-lit porch but saw nothing out of place. "You said *sneaking out of the house*. Did you see him inside my place?" Did she need to call 911?

Instead of explaining her cryptic comments, Miss Allan hugged the gold fur ball to her chest. Her eyes had narrowed to study Gigi's ragged appearance. "Are you all right, dear? You look a bit rattled. Why are you all dressed up? Did you have a date?"

Goose bumps prickled Gigi's skin as she looked up and down the street for any sign that could explain away this uncomfortable feeling of being the object of unwanted attention. It was the same sense of creepy she'd felt when Gary had spied on the last of her interview with Hud. Could he have gotten here before her? Did she even know what kind of car Gary drove?

"Miss Allan, was the driver parked in my driveway or just turning around?"

"Did he dump you?" The older woman went on as if Gigi hadn't spoken. "Men these days don't appreciate a quiet girl like you."

The woman was lonely and making conversation. Gigi typically indulged her because she understood that kind of isolation. But if she couldn't get the information that would ease her own concern, then she wanted to go inside and check the house for herself, call the police again if necessary, then get into a hot shower and sleep for about ten hours. She retreated to her car, moving toward the steps of the stone porch. "It wasn't a date. I had a work thing this evening. If you'll excuse me, I really want to see if my house is okay."

She stopped when she realized her neighbor was following her.

"You work too much, Virginia. I bet men would ask you out if you did something with your hair. And wore clothes that show your cleavage." Miss Allan gasped an apology before resting her hand on Gigi's arm and tilting her face up to hers. "I'm so sorry, dear. I didn't mean to point out any inadequacies. You know, you can buy a bra that has gel in the cups. That'll give you a little more oomph upstairs. Men like that."

If her boss hadn't been murdered and her car wasn't wrecked, then getting dating advice from her eighty-five-year-old neighbor was a strong indicator that Gigi's night couldn't get any worse.

"Thank you for watching the place, Miss Allan." Gigi's patience for small talk had zeroed out, along with her self-esteem and flagging energy. She'd had one too many shocks tonight to handle anything but solitude right now. "You don't want Izzy to catch a chill in this night air. Good night."

If Miss Allan wanted to say anything more, Gigi wasn't waiting around to hear it. "Good night, dear."

Since nothing seemed to be disturbed on the front porch, Gigi slipped inside, turning the dead bolt behind her and heading past her bedroom and living room at the front of the house. In the kitchen, she spared a moment to peek through the curtains of the side window to make sure Miss Allan and Izzy got safely inside their house before she flipped on the light and took off her shoes. Her toes throbbed with thanks at being released from their high-heeled prison, although she shivered at the cold tiles beneath the soles of her feet. Then again, maybe it wasn't the floor that chilled her.

She set her backpack on the peninsula counter and made sure the dead bolt was still in place on the back door before moving through the rest of the house, including Tammy's loft-bedroom suite. Although she found a torn screen in the laundry room, no one seemed to have gotten in. The television was still in the living room, her computer and Tammy's gaming and music systems were still in their bedrooms. If there had been an attempted break-in, then maybe Miss Allan's watchful eyes or Gigi's late arrival had scared him away before he could take anything.

She was safe. Alone, but safe. And alone was better than having an intruder to keep her company, right? Alone was better than facing reporters or being bullied by Evgeni Zajac or *darling*ed by Gary Haack.

With her naked toes protesting the chill of the wood-and-tile floors, she returned to the kitchen and picked up the teakettle on the stove. A hot cup of tea might chase this frosty mood away. She'd get the water started, then take a quick shower and change into her pajamas.

She was leaning against the edge of the copper farm sink, filling the kettle under the faucet when she noticed the blood that was still on her hands. A mix of disgust and grief squeezed in her chest and she set the kettle aside to thrust her fingers beneath the water instead. Pumping a palmful of soap from the dispenser beside the sink, she lathered up her hands until she could no longer see the skin. Although a crime-scene technician had scraped beneath her nails and the paramedic had given her a disinfectant wipe to wash up at the ambulance, there was still evidence of Ian's last moments staining her fingers. Increasing the water's temperature, she rubbed at her cuticles and scraped the bristles of the cleaning brush she used on the dishes beneath her nails.

She rinsed and soaped again and again until her hands blurred in front of her eyes. Gigi had lost people she cared about before—most notably her parents who'd died in a car wreck. Her father had perished instantly, and her mother had held on for two more days in the hospital until she, too, had succumbed to her injuries. At that time, she'd had a master's thesis she needed to finish so she could get a job to support herself and her younger sister. There had been funeral arrangements to make, insurance to deal with. She'd shut down her emotions then because it had been the only way she could get through it all. She'd become strong because she had to be. Tammy had needed her. No one else was going to take care of them.

But she was so damn tired of being sensible and strong and dealing with the trials life threw into her path again and again. Just because she *could* deal didn't mean she always wanted to be the one who had to.

*If it hasn't hit you yet, it will.* Hud had been right.

Logically, she knew the shock was wearing off, and irrational thoughts were sneaking past her broken defenses. The blankness that had gotten her through tonight was crumbling away, allowing the grief, helplessness and rage to bombard her emotional barriers. She tried to focus on some of the good that had happened tonight, like the hug from Hana Nowak, her neighbor's concern, Hudson Kramer putting up a wall of muscle between her and Gary's unwanted touch, walking her to her car like a gentleman or calling her by that silly nickname, G. But she couldn't recall the warmth of Hud's hand at her back or feel the softness of his jacket clutched in her fingers or hear the deep timbre of his laughter soothing her senses. She was alone. She was frightened. She was lost. And it seemed no amount of logical thinking or silly fantasy could give her the comfort she needed.

Shutting off the water, Gigi sank to the floor and let the tears come. More than the physical trauma of being attacked, the emotional trauma of all she'd dealt with tonight washed over her in waves.

Ian Lombard had looked out for her. He'd hired her for a job she loved, advised her when she struggled with her teaching. *You're my prize, Gigi*, he'd told her after the first time the university had honored Ian and his team for their groundbreaking work. He'd meant something to her, and he'd died beneath her hands.

He'd argued a lot, too. With his wife. His staff. University officials. Yes, he'd abandoned her tonight at the reception, but he'd never turned those volatile words on her.

She remembered Ian gasping for breath to speak to her as blood gurgled in his throat. *My prize...smarter than me.* He'd valued her in ways that few people did.

Her body went limp and her sinuses burned. Tears rolled down her cheeks, singeing her skin and fogging up her glasses.

She sat there on the floor in front of the sink, her knees hugged to her chest, quietly crying until her cheeks felt chapped and her nose ran. She sat there until the tears ran out and there was no emotion left. She was exhausted. Her eyes felt gritty. But she could think. A little.

First of all, she needed a tissue. She could stand up and reach the paper towels. But her legs felt as weak as her brain. How many times had she hidden a tissue into the pockets of her sweater, to give her something to work between her fingers, dispelling the nervous energy she felt when she got self-conscious in front of a lecture hall or conference table? Pretending the blood stains weren't there, marring the sweater her mother had knitted for her years ago, she reached into her left pocket. There was her phone. She reached into the right pocket. There was a tissue. But her victory was short-lived.

Feeling a tinge of panic, she dug through both pockets again.

She was missing something.

The note. Ian's note.

The scrap of paper he'd been so desperate for her to take.

*Find... Finish it.*

"Finish what?" she murmured, grabbing the edge of the sink and pulling herself to her feet.

She stumbled over to the counter and rummaged through her backpack, unzipping each pocket before dumping out everything but her laptop. What had she done with that note? It had been Ian's last gift to her, and she'd lost it.

Or maybe it had been Ian's last cry for help. *Finish it.*

"He was giving me a message." One that only her brain could understand and figure out.

A clue to his killer? A motive?

Gigi checked her discarded shoes, unrolled the cuffs of her sweater for any sign of the crumpled note. She tried to recall the symbols she'd seen on that paper. *A. U. N. O. 3.* Ian often encoded his notes to keep curious eyes from copying his work until he was ready to reveal it. But would a dying man waste his final moments writing in code? She shook her head. Not random letters. Not even code. Au. "Gold." $NO_3$. "Nitrate. Gold nitrate." It was a scientific formula. Similar to one they'd been developing for a small-size, large-capacity power cell to drive industrial computers, one that could also be adapted to other uses in the medical and military fields. Only, they hadn't been able to shrink the capacitor to their target size yet and still maintain the control function they wanted. The formula Ian had given her had been slightly different. And definitely incomplete. *Finish it.*

She'd have to remember the rest of the formula or develop it herself if she couldn't find that piece of paper.

She paused a moment in her frantic search. The new formula—the new device—would be worth millions to anyone who wanted to revolutionize the computer industry. Maybe even more to the person who could weaponize their design and sell it on the black market.

Motive. Millions, if not billions, of motives for killing a man.

"Where is that damn paper?" She unzipped the cosmetics bag where she carried some medications, lip balm and a compact. She opened the compact. She looked in the bottle of ibuprofen, even though she knew she hadn't stashed Ian's note in either location. She unzipped her billfold, checked the cash there, sorted through her debit and credit cards and ID. "What…?" She pulled her driver's license from behind her bank card. "Why are you here?"

She slipped her license back into the see-through pocket where she normally kept it. The punch cards she kept for gasoline and a campus coffee shop were in the wrong pocket, too. Hud had said the police had searched her bag before she left the university. Would they rearrange the contents inside?

Or had someone else searched through her backpack?

That chill crept up her spine with renewed strength

as she backed away from her things on the counter. She threaded her fingers through her hair, even relishing the slight tug of pain at the back of her scalp. "What is happening to me?"

Whoever had searched her bag, read her license, would know her address. If that person wanted Ian's formula, and thought she had it—if that person had taken the note, but realized it was unfinished work and believed she could complete the formula—if that person thought she understood their motive for killing Ian...

*Trust no one*, Ian had warned her.

Gigi quickly stuffed everything back into her backpack and closed it. There were too many reasons for someone to search her house, to follow her home— too many reasons why she might be the key to solving Ian's murder.

She bypassed her black heels and slipped her feet into the grass-stained tennis shoes she wore when she worked in the yard and headed out the door to her car. She started the engine and saw the light in Miss Allan's bedroom come on. She'd come home late, been nearly run down, and now she was leaving again in the middle of the night. She was really giving her neighbor some juicy gossip to obsess over.

But she needed to talk to Hud. She needed to tell him what was happening.

He wanted details? She had plenty of them to share.

And he would listen. Even if he thought she was nuts, he would still listen.

He was a good man. He might even be her friend.

Forget that he'd been her fantasy for two years.

The most important detail to her right now was that Hudson Kramer made her feel safe.

# Chapter Six

Tuning out the familiar buzz of noise around him in the precinct offices, Hudson stared at the sketch of the Lombard crime scene he'd made in his notebook, wondering what was wrong with this picture. The first forty-eight hours were crucial to a murder investigation, and he was burning through that time without anything but a suspected murder weapon he couldn't find to show for it.

What was wrong with this picture was that Virginia Brennan was smack-dab in the middle of it. He couldn't imagine anyone less suited for the violence of that crime scene or less equipped to understand the secrets and motives that would lead someone to commit murder. She was too shy to deal with the ensuing chaos, too traumatized by the loss of her boss and friend to cope with the wham-bam push to move as quickly as possible to find answers and arrest a suspect.

What was wrong with *him* was that he kept thinking about the statuesque redhead with the big, soulful eyes instead of concentrating on the clues that wouldn't fit together in any sensible way. Some pointed to premeditation while others indicated a crime of opportunity spurred by anger. Too many suspects had motive for killing Lombard. And while Keir was tracking down which of those suspects would have also had the opportunity to be at the tech lab with Dr. Lombard, there was no way to eliminate any of them until other pieces started falling into place.

Gigi had no business being this close to a murder investigation.

And he had no business resurrecting that ill-advised attraction he'd put out of his mind these past two years. The quiet, complicated professor couldn't be more wrong for a streetwise smart-ass like him. Or maybe he was having trouble accepting that he was wrong for her. It would be his dumb luck to fall for someone he couldn't have. She was class and culture and cutting-edge science, and he was…not.

Buzzing his lips with a regretful sigh, Hud glanced up from his desk in the bullpen at the Fourth Precinct office. With most of B shift out on patrol, there were only the desk sergeant near the elevators and a handful of detectives and uniformed officers scattered throughout their cubicles on the main floor. The offices of the precinct captain and other command ranks were dark and locked up and would probably stay that way until Monday morning. Most of the men and women on duty were typing up reports or shootin' the breeze around cubicle walls, or in the break room drinking coffee and eating the night shift's equivalent of an afternoon snack. A few, like his partner at the desk across from his, were fixated on computer screens as they tracked down leads on cases.

Although he had a working knowledge of computers, Hud tended to go old school, writing down his observations and insights on an investigation by hand rather than texting notes to his computer. He liked the visceral feel of putting pen to paper. There was something about the tactile experience that flowed up his arm and triggered the thought processes in his brain.

Only, tonight, his brain was misfiring. Instead of piecing together details on the murder, the only thing he could see when he tapped his pen against the paper was a waterfall of long auburn hair and dove-gray eyes that had shown him panic, sadness and, if he wasn't mistaken, heat when he'd caught her staring at him on the bench outside the Williams University Technology Building.

Damn. Had he really forgotten that whole sexy librarian vibe Gigi Brennan had charmed him with two years ago when he'd rescued her from being abandoned at the Shamrock Bar? It wasn't like she had a killer rack or was a cute kind of pretty like her sister or even had an easy-to-hang-with personality.

Maybe it was because she wasn't like any woman he'd met that she'd made such an impression on him.

She'd been so serious about learning the rules of playing pool, so curious why he'd chosen a bottled beer over the draft his partner had. She'd explained the advantages and disadvantages of the fluorescent lighting above the pool table and expounded on why men were more drawn to her gregarious sister than to a shy, self-avowed nerd like her. And then she'd leaned over the corner of the table with her bottom bobbing in the air beside him to get a different angle on an impossible shot, and all the blood in his bemused brain had rushed straight to his groin. She'd also earned his undying admiration when her last striped ball had caromed off two sides and sunk into the corner pocket.

Her victorious smile that night—because she'd mastered the skill, not because she'd defeated him—had hit him with the same surprising force as the way she'd smiled tonight after he'd gotten rid of her pesky coworkers and first called her G. Making Gigi Brennan smile made him feel good, made him feel like an able-bodied man instead of a second-string sidekick to men who topped six feet and knew how to charm the ladies.

There was something adorable about the way she peeked over her glasses to make eye contact when they were close. And those legs—long and lean, nicely curved—man, they went on forever. The sequins and bulky sweater hadn't been the right look for her, but he'd love to see her in a slinky pencil skirt that stopped right above the dimple in her right knee, like she'd worn that night at the bar. Along with a button-up blouse that he could unbutton. Or a shapeless white lab coat with some lacy lingerie on underneath it. He had a feeling that Gigi was full of surprises beneath that introverted exterior.

Surprises like the way she'd thrown herself into that kiss two years ago.

Hud absentmindedly flipped through the pages in his notebook, seeing images from the past rather than what was right in front of him. His blood simmered as his thoughts fully engaged on the wrong topic. He'd been a little taken aback by Gigi's eager response to his good-night kiss at the end of that weird, un-planned date night. The heady rush of being desired had fueled his ego and soothed something needy buried deep inside him. That was so not a kiss between casual acquaintances or even friends. Gigi's grabby hands and welcoming passion had fueled something else inside him, too.

For about twenty seconds, he'd savored everything the woman was willing to give him. Had urged her to give even more. And she had. Her inexperienced mouth had been hot and sweet, and oh, so ready to learn. Her hands had traveled over his face and shoulders, pinching the skin underneath as she dragged herself closer, as if she couldn't get enough of the taste and feel of him.

It was that twenty-first second when he'd come to his senses and remembered he was supposed to be her safe escort home, not some sex-starved wingman who'd take advantage of her awkward innocence.

It was about twenty-five seconds into saying good-night when he reminded himself that university professor Virginia Brennan—the shy intellectual with the conservative clothes and social naivete—was way out of his league for a working-class Joe like him. She was big-city born and raised while he was half hillbilly from the Ozarks. She had multiple college degrees, and had mentioned scholarships and early graduations, while he'd enlisted in the police academy to get a job to support his siblings. He had to work his way through night school to earn his degree and finally make detective three years after the other members of his academy class had.

Gigi was interesting, a puzzle of contradictions he didn't understand. She was unintentionally funny and vulnerable in a way she probably didn't even realize, which, of course, triggered every overprotective bone in his body. Plus, he figured he'd have to be about twice as smart as he was to be half as smart as her. There were lowlifes on the streets in No-Man's-Land he had more in common with.

And yet she'd turned that polite kiss into something heated and raw and…

With his feverish frustration and useless fantasies about to blow out his ears, Hud pocketed his notebook and rolled his chair away from his desk. He shrugged into his jacket and tapped the desktop to get Keir's attention. "Hey. I'm going to take a short drive to clear my head. You want anything while I'm out?"

Keir looked up from the ME's preliminary report he'd been studying. "I'm good." He pointed to the data on his computer screen. "You were right about the whiskey bottle. Niall said he found alcohol in several of the wound tracts."

Keir's ME brother hadn't wasted any time getting them the information they needed to confirm Hud's suspicions. "Great. The only bottle on the scene was sealed and clean. I guess that means doing some Dumpster diving to find a broken bottle. Shouldn't be too many of those around the city."

Keir laughed at the snark that colored Hud's voice. "Hey, it's your lead. *You* get to dive in."

Hud's mood lightened a little bit at his friend's teasing. "Whatever happened to teamwork?"

Waving his hand in front of himself, Keir pointed

out his spit-and-polish perfection. "Suit and tie." Then he pointed to Hud. "Hillbilly chic…" His gaze narrowed and moved past Hud. "What's she doing here?"

Hud turned, fully expecting to see Keir's wife, or possibly Keir's sister or stepgrandmother, showing up with some kind of family emergency. Instead, he saw Gigi Brennan at the sergeant's desk, signing a clipboard and looping a visitor's badge around her neck. She still wore the same sequins-and-sweater look from earlier, although she'd traded in her heels for a normal pair of tennis shoes. Had his wandering thoughts somehow conjured her here?

"Close your mouth, Kramer," Keir advised him, rising to his feet. "You finished the interview, right?"

Hud's surprise was quickly replaced with a wary feeling that raised the hairs on the back of his neck. "I took her statement and sent her home." Had that pig Professor Haack forced his company on her again? The urgency in her movements clearly indicated something was wrong. "She shouldn't be here."

"She's making a beeline right to you, buddy."

Hud waved off the desk sergeant who had picked up the phone to alert him to her arrival and moved forward as Gigi zigzagged her way through the desks. Without those high heels, he could look her straight in the eye—hers were red-rimmed, determined and focused squarely on him. "G? What are you doing here?"

"Did you find a note at the crime scene?" She started talking before she stopped in front of him. "It would have been on Ian's university letterhead. Handwritten. Crumpled up. Stained with his blood."

"What are you talking about?"

Her words spewed out in a panicked rush. "I remembered something. Key evidence, I think. Except I lost it. Or someone took it from me. Ian *did* say something important to me before he—" her gaze darted past him to Keir "—before he…died." She turned to the break room, then to her right, seeing the uniformed officers and other detectives pause their conversations and lift their focuses from their computers. He could see her mentally counting all the faces staring curiously at them. Her hands tightened around the straps of her backpack and her words faltered. "Um… I… Why are there so many people here? It's the middle of the night."

He probably shouldn't remind her that this was light in terms of personnel. "KC's a big city. The police work around the clock. Somebody's always on duty. Friday nights keep us especially busy."

She touched the temples of her glasses as if they needed adjusting. Nervous habit? Or coping mechanism? "Why are they looking at me?"

"Don't pay any attention to those yahoos. We don't get a lot of visitors this time of night who aren't in handcuffs." He didn't want to mention that the dried blood on her sweater might have some of them concerned about needing their help. He tried to ease some of the tension tightening her posture with another joke. "And the only time a lady stops by to see me is when my sisters are in town."

"You don't have a girlfriend?"

"Not at the moment. Not for a long time."

"Why not?"

"Good question." Women got what they needed from him, and then they set him aside and moved on. He guessed she wasn't really looking for his dating history, though. Gigi's nerves had kicked in and her brain had shut down. "Hey." Let his coworkers start the inevitable gossip. Gigi was upset, and she'd come to him for help. A damsel in distress had always been his Achilles' heel. Hud slid his fingers along the line of her jaw, cupping the side of her face. When she startled, he anchored his fingertips at the nape of her neck before she could pull away. Her hand came up to wind around his wrist, but her attention had shifted out of her head and back to him. Damn if that wasn't another thing he liked about her—her instinct to reach out to him and hold on. He stroked his thumb across her cheek, noting the pink irritation around her eyes. "You've been crying. Are you feeling okay? Any symptoms of a concussion?"

She shook her head. "Physically, I'll be fine. But you were right. You said the shock would wear off and the grief would hit me, and it did."

"I'm sorry, G."

She released him as suddenly as she'd latched on to tug up the hem of her sweater and pull out a wad of tissues that she waved in front of him. "But I'm glad I had that crying jag because I was looking for these when I remembered the note."

"The one you lost at the crime scene?"

"The one that Ian gave me."

"Lombard gave you a note?"

"Before he died." She stuffed the tissues back into her pocket. "He couldn't really talk, so he wrote it down. He was adamant that I take it. I tucked it into my sweater and now it's gone. I don't know if I lost it or if it was stolen. Somebody rifled through my bag. Maybe the killer was looking for it. I know the police searched it. That's why I hoped you had it?"

Hud shook his head. He didn't have three college degrees, but he wasn't stupid. Still, this conversation wasn't making much sense. He took Gigi by the elbow and turned toward the meeting rooms lining the walls at the far side of the bullpen. "Let's go someplace a little more private. Then you can start at the beginning."

"I'll bring you two some coffee," Keir offered, trading a nod with Hud as they walked past. His partner obviously shared his concerns about this late-night visit. He wasn't sure what key piece of evidence Gigi thought she'd had. But the fact that she was now missing it had her worried. And that worried him.

Hud opened the door to the first empty room and led Gigi to a chair at the head of the table. He crossed to the window to glare at the nosy officers who'd moved to keep him and Gigi in their line of sight before pulling the blinds shut on the *Hudson-Kramer's-with-a-woman?* shock on their faces. "I said to call me if you remembered anything else about Lombard's murder. I could have looked up what we've catalogued from the crime scene so far for you. You didn't need to come downtown in the middle of the night like this."

"I didn't have your number," Gigi answered. "Besides, there was that SUV that spooked me, so I just wanted to get out of the house."

His hand fisted around the cord. "What SUV?"

"The one that sideswiped my car. One that possibly followed me home."

"Someone hit your car?" He spun around. She'd already taken one blow to the head. "Were you hurt? Who followed you?"

"I don't think so. He was backing out of my driveway—"

"He was at your house?" Hud pulled out his cell phone to put in a call to Patrol. "Did you get a plate number?"

"It was too dark, and he was going too fast. He didn't have his lights on. He was probably just turning around. Not all the houses on my street have driveways."

"Can you describe the car? The driver?"

"Black? An SUV. The car had tinted windows. I could barely make out the outline of a driver and then he was gone." She raked her fingers into her hair to push it off her face, wincing when she must have tugged against the goose egg on her scalp. "I thought he'd broken in, but I think he just vandalized my screen. And I don't see how someone following me could possibly get to my house before me."

The list continued and he was getting pissed— at whoever was terrorizing this woman tonight. He didn't for one damn minute think she was crazy or that this had anything to do with the blow to her head. He pulled a chair down to the corner of the table and sat right in front of her. "Let me get this straight— a car ran into you? You should have called me right then. Or 911. You were followed from the campus? You think someone tried to break in—"

"I couldn't find any broken locks or windows to confirm that theory."

"—went through your bag and stole Lombard's note out of your pocket? Damn it, G. A man was murdered. You were assaulted. Stuff like that isn't supposed to happen to a woman like you."

He couldn't tell if it was his harsh tone, spelling out the accusations she'd listed or the fact he was sitting close enough to inhale the alcohol and disinfectant and something fainter that was soft like vanilla clinging to her clothes and skin that widened her eyes and made her fall silent. She stuck her hands into her pockets and leaned back in her chair. Away from him.

Oh, hell. The last thing he needed was for her to be afraid of him. "I'm sorry. I didn't mean to…"

His apology drifted off when her gaze darted to the whiteboard on the wall and she pushed to her feet. She picked up a marker and started writing—symbols, numbers, letters that didn't form words—while she spoke. "Whoever attacked me must have overheard what Ian was saying to me, and wanted that information for himself."

"What are you doing?" he asked, wondering if this was another shy person thing to keep her hands busy so talking or being alone with him wouldn't make her so nervous.

"Writing down everything I remember from Ian's note."

Hud rose more slowly and circled the table, not wanting to frighten her into shutting down again. Pushing a chair aside, he leaned his hips back against the table and folded his arms over his chest. "You think that note is the reason Lombard was killed?"

"Possibly." She erased two numbers with the side of her hand, then wrote them again, reversing the order. Wow. All those letters and math-looking symbols meant nothing to him. But apparently it was a language in which Gigi was fluent. She stepped back for a moment to survey the board before pointing to the top line of her work. "This is part of a formula."

"For something your lab was working on?"

"For something revolutionary if it's what I think it is."

"Is it worth a lot of money?"

Despite her obvious fatigue, her whole body hummed with energy as she analyzed what she'd written. He knew a handful of scary-smart people—and then there was whatever was going on inside Gigi's head. Like an athlete who was in the zone and running the perfect race, it was kind of hot to see the wheels churning inside her brain and feel the intelligence radiating out of every pore. "Potentially. If the equation was completed. A prototype would have to be built. We have the materials at the lab. If the design works, it could be worth a fortune."

"A prototype for what?"

She spun around to face him, her soft eyes sparkling with a silvery gleam. Oh, yeah. Brainpower was definitely hot. "Think of the biggest computers in the world—that run multinational corporations or communication networks." She waved her arms in a big circle. "Computers that fill warehouses and underground bunkers and need their own power plant to run them." She tugged on his wrist to uncross his arms, then placed the marker in his hand. "Then shrink it down to fit in the palm of your hand."

He looked at the board. "That's what all that is? A computer?"

"The power cell to run one. Ian must have cracked the code. But I can't tell if he didn't finish the equation—or he just didn't finish writing it down before he died." He wondered if she even knew her fingers had remained wrapped around his over the marker and that she'd given him a subtle squeeze before she pulled away to examine the whiteboard again. "I don't know what this line of numbers means. Phone number? Bank account? Maybe he encrypted a message to me."

"While he was dying?" In Hud's experience, people who were dying took the time to share hopes or regrets, not play scrambled communication games.

"Ian could be a little paranoid. I got pretty good at deciphering his notes." She visibly shivered and hugged her arms around herself again. "Except, I have no idea what it means."

"Could it be a password?" Hud suggested, trying to come up with a more practical explanation. "If it's a phone number, it would have to be a foreign country exchange." When she glanced back at him, he winked. *I know a couple of things, too, sweetheart.* "Too many numbers to be local."

"Dr. Zajac and his wife are from Lukinburg. They travel back and forth between our countries a couple of times a month."

"And you told me Lombard's wife is studying abroad this semester."

Gigi nodded. The silvery light that had brightened her eyes a few moments earlier was fading. "Do you think he wanted me to call Doris? Tell his wife he loved her? Or apologize for his past mistakes? I'm not good at stuff like that."

"I can plug in the numbers and run a quick search. See if a phone number pops up." He copied down everything she had written in his notebook. Wait. *Part of a formula?* "This isn't complete?" His instincts going on high alert, he pushed away from the table. Following her across town? Hitting her car? No way was any of that random. "Maybe the killer thinks you know something he couldn't get from Lombard and now he's after you."

"After me?"

He rubbed his hand up and down her arm, alarmed by the trembling he felt there. That rush of energy that had propelled her to the whiteboard was rapidly dissipating. She was going to crash soon. Crash hard. "Look, I don't mean to scare you, but—"

"No. That makes sense." She sank into the closest chair. "Ian said I was smarter than he was—he knew I could figure this out. He wanted me to complete his work one last time. If I had access to his notes, I could decipher them. I know how his mind worked. I could probably do it without his notes. If I had a few days."

"Would anyone else be able to finish the formula and build a prototype?"

"Possibly Dr. Zajac."

"The foreign professor who likes to argue?"

She nodded.

"What about his wife?"

"Hana?" Gigi shook her head. "She's a translator. Her only knowledge of physics and engineering would come from observation. She transcribes his notes, sits in on staff meetings. She's familiar with the jargon, but I doubt she could apply what she's learned into a device that could actually work." Her lips tightened with a frown. "If he had the equation in front of him, Gary could build the prototype."

He tried not to grin at the venom behind her tone. He wondered what Haack had done to Gigi to make her have such a low opinion of the guy. But when he saw her shiver, any idea of being amused vanished. Hud shrugged off his jacket and draped it around her shoulders. Kneeling in front of her, he pulled the jacket together in front of her slim body and continued to rub his hands up and down her arms, willing his body heat to keep her going a little while longer.

"Hang in there, G. We'll figure this out." He glanced up at the board and shrugged. "Well, you'll figure *that* out. I'll take care of the bad guys."

"Like a team? Brains and Brawn?"

"Yeah. I'll be the muscle head. Probably work out better for us both that way." When even that self-deprecating joke didn't earn a smile, he caught a lock of long, auburn hair that had fallen in front of her glasses and brushed it back behind her ear. It was as smooth and silky to the touch as he remembered from that night he'd sunk his fingers into her hair and kissed her. The tactile memory triggered a visceral response deep in his gut, heating his blood even as he felt her chilled skin beneath his fingertips. He cupped his hand against the side of her neck, wishing he had the right to pull her into his arms and show her how that brawny strength could shield her and support her through the physical, mental and emotional turmoil she'd been through. "You've had a long night. You should be home soaking in a hot bath or sleeping by now."

"I don't like baths. It takes too long to fill the tub, and my skin gets pruney. A shower is much more efficient."

Not helping with the errant hormones. The pruney comment made him notice her skin. It'd be a shame to do anything that might mar that smooth, creamy expanse. Despite her dark red hair, there was nary a freckle he could see across her cheeks or long neck. That alabaster skin was unblemished all the way down to...

He thanked the fates for the soft knock at the door and pushed to his feet to see Keir enter. His partner handed Hud a cup of coffee and set another, along with a handful of sugars and creamers, on the table in front of Gigi. "I brewed a fresh pot. Wasn't sure how you take yours."

Unaware of the questioning look Keir gave Hud as he took in the leather jacket around her shoulders and his rapid retreat from the witness he was supposed to be interrogating, Gigi pried the lid off her coffee cup and dumped in two creamers. "Usually I drink tea, but I need something stronger to keep me going tonight. Thank you."

"My pleasure." Keir pulled back the front of his

jacket to prop his hands on his hips as he studied the writing that filled the whiteboard. "What's this? Are we having science class?"

Hud drank a sip of the potent brew to tamp down those crazy flashes of desire Gigi stirred in him and think like a detective again. "It could be the reason Lombard was killed."

"What's it mean?" Keir asked.

"It means whoever builds what this formula has designed can make a powerful weapon that could be controlled remotely, or bring down a satellite or communication grid from their basement, or run an entire hospital from the back of a truck, making the owner an awful lot of money—legitimately. Even more on the black market." He glanced over at Gigi, huddling in his jacket and warming her fingers around the coffee cup. "Is that about right?"

She nodded. "You're a good listener." She lifted her gaze to Keir. "Of course, our lab wasn't designing the minicapacitor for criminal applications, but that's motive, isn't it?"

"That's a hell of a lot of motive," Keir agreed.

The more important piece of information Hud had gotten tonight was that Gigi was in danger. "Lombard gave this information to Professor Brennan, and now it's missing. She was assaulted at the crime scene. Somebody rammed her car tonight. And she believes someone followed her home and was casing her house." He slid his notebook across the table to Keir. "Her address is in here. Send a black-and-white over there to keep an eye on the place until I can get there. I'm driving Gigi home."

"You are?" She tilted her chin to him. "What about my car? I'll be stranded again."

"But you won't be alone." Hud closed the lid on his disposable cup, prepared for any argument she might give him on this. "Right now, you need sleep. Monday, we're going to take pictures of the damage to your car, file a police report and send it to your insurance. I've got a shop guy who works on my truck. We'll take your car to him once we've got the paperwork done."

"I have to go to the lab tomorrow—later this morning, I guess—to inventory supplies and equipment, meet with the research team." She braced her hand on the tabletop and stood. "You're giving up your time to chauffeur me around? What about your investigation?"

"You *are* the investigation." Not that he thought she had the strength to protest much, but he wasn't going to argue with her on this. He turned back to Keir. "It's not much to go on, but I also want you to put out an APB for a black SUV with tinted windows. The paint job will probably be scratched up from hitting Gigi's car."

"I'm on it." Keir snapped a picture of the address with his phone, backing Hud's plan without question. He returned the notebook and took several pictures of the whiteboard. "I'll copy these into our case file while you head on out. The lab said they'd get me some preliminary results yet tonight. I'll keep you posted."

"I recommend we keep Gigi's name out of the press for now. Although, the killer may already have a bead on her as the key to all this." He waved his hand toward the whiteboard.

"Agreed. If you need anything else, let me know. I could send my brother or sister over to help keep watch if you need to sleep."

Keir's oldest brother and younger sister were both detectives. His middle brother worked at the crime lab and was probably finishing up the autopsy on Ian Lombard right now. "Thanks. I'll be okay tonight. I may need someone to spell me later."

"One of us will be there," Keir promised.

Hud held out his hand to Gigi and waited for her to circle around the table to join him. "Shall we?"

When she tried to return his jacket, he held it so that she could slide her arms into the sleeves instead. The fact that she didn't protest him railroading her into leaving with him was a sign of how exhausted she must be.

Keir stopped Hud on the way out. "Professor, you mind giving me a minute with my partner?"

"It's Gigi." She offered him a weary smile. "And no. I'll find a restroom and meet you out here."

Hud gave her directions to the closest facility and watched her until she disappeared inside. Once they were alone, he faced his partner. "All right. Let's hear the lecture."

Keir didn't waste any time getting to the concern that had been stamped on his face. "What are you doing, Hud? There's no protection order on this case. You didn't even want to take lead with this witness. Now you're spending the night at her house? Promising her 24/7 security? Captain Hendricks wants us to solve a homicide, not babysit a woman who's gotten under your skin. We haven't even been on this case twenty-four hours."

"I've known her for two years. She needs me."

"She needs a friend."

No doubt. With Gigi's social anxiety and her sister out of town, there probably weren't many people she'd call on at a time like this. "Well, then that's what I'll be. She's alone and she's scared, and I don't think she gets people. She'd be easy to hurt. Easy for our perp to victimize and take advantage of. Until we arrest a suspect, this guy's going to keep coming after whatever is locked up inside that brain of hers."

"She's not the one I'm worried about." Keir's mouth twisted with concern. "I've seen you do this a hundred times. Running in to save the day. Giving up a little piece of your heart because a woman needs you. How many pieces you got left?"

"Enough to get G through this. Enough to keep her safe." Hud raked all ten fingers through his hair and muttered a curse. His partner knew him better than any other man on the planet. Keir wasn't the only detective to see the pattern repeating itself. "Look, I know I've had nothin' but bad luck with the ladies. Maybe it's time to give up on the idea of forever. But I won't give up on right now. And right now, Virginia Brennan needs me."

"She needs a cop."

"I *am* a cop."

Keir considered his argument for a moment, then nodded. "And a damn good one." He reached out to shake Hud's hand and squeeze his shoulder. "However this plays out, I've got your back, partner."

Hud nodded. "Works for me."

## Chapter Seven

Hud snapped one last picture of the window into Gigi's laundry room before the uniformed officer beside him propped a piece of plywood over the cut screen. "I appreciate the help."

"Not a problem, sir." He radioed his partner, who'd stayed inside the house with Gigi while they'd swept the yard and surrounding area. "We'll cruise by the place again before our shift is done in the morning," he added before striding away.

"Thanks." Hud debated whether or not he should tell Gigi about the pry marks that bent the strike plate on her back door. If the perp had used something heavy enough to leave those marks, then he'd probably only been seconds away from switching tactics and breaking through the window to get inside. And if he'd been inside already when Gigi got home... Hud had seen too much to not be able to imagine how a lone woman discovering an intruder with a crowbar and a cutting blade might end up.

He rolled his neck and reached up to massage the tension gathering beneath his collar. What had stopped the perp from the easy break-in in the first place? Someone willing to commit murder wouldn't hesitate to break a window. The juxtaposition of crime elements here was just as perplexing as the clues from the scene of Lombard's murder.

How much did he share with her about his investigation? Hud wanted Gigi to be aware of the danger she was facing, but with sunrise coming in a couple of hours, he didn't want to upset her so much that she couldn't grab a little sleep before she called her staff in for an emergency meeting, and they looked through Lombard's files and computer.

The perceptive squint behind her glasses when she opened the door rendered his internal debate moot. "Tell me what you found."

Hud scraped his palm across the stubble of his jaw and offered her a wry grin. "There's no sugarcoatin' anything with you, is there."

"I need to understand everything that's happening to me. I don't function well when my mind's a jumble."

She locked the door before heading into her kitchen. The entire room smelled like potent coffee and something spicy, but it couldn't mask the scent of warm vanilla that emanated from her damp hair and skin after her shower. She'd coiled that brick-colored hair on top of her head and wore flannel pajama pants, bright green socks and a gray hoodie over a T-shirt. She should have looked frumpy, or like a teenage girl in that shapeless getup. Instead, all he saw was *sexy librarian* with those loose tendrils falling from her up-swept hair clinging to her long neck, and that sweet, heart-shaped butt framed in faded plaid flannel.

Although he'd told her she should go to bed while he checked her security, she'd insisted that she wanted to stay up long enough to wash her sweater and wrap it in a towel to let it dry. Although he got the feeling that she was normally fine on her own, and would appreciate a quiet house, he couldn't blame her for not wanting to be alone until her boss's killer was caught. Or, judging by the legal pad loaded with equations and scribbles she'd left sitting on the countertop by her mug of tea, she didn't intend to rest until she completed Lombard's formula.

"Hud?"

The moment his gaze focused on hers, she adjusted her glasses in that habitual gesture, waiting for his answer. He hung his jacket on the back of a chair and adjusted his gun on his belt. "You did have a visitor. Somebody was looking for a way into your house. Either the locks were solid enough to thwart him or he got interrupted before he could get in. Officer Cho and I patched it up."

"When we first moved here, I was a child. It wasn't the best neighborhood, but it was close to my advanced prep school. Dad installed steel-framed windows and steel doors with dead bolts. We never had a break-in growing up." She filled a plate with crudités and cookies. "Plus, Miss Allan next door has insomnia and likes to keep an eye on the neighborhood. She was up when I got home. Maybe he saw her at her window. Or turning on her lights was enough to chase him off."

"Possibly." He was glad to see an empty plate on the countertop peninsula, indicating that she'd eaten a snack to sustain her. He pulled out a stool there and sat down. "I don't subscribe to coincidence enough to believe it was a random break-in attempt. Whoever was here will be back with better tools. Or he'll find another way to get to you."

"Because he thinks I have the rest of Ian's formula?"

He nodded to the yellow legal pad. "Or he thinks he can convince you to complete the work for him."

She set the plate in front of him, giving him the choice of a healthy or sugary snack. "How would they convince me? Bribery? I don't need the money. They won't kill me because what they need is inside my brain."

"You saw what they did to Lombard. There are ways to bend you to someone's will. Torture? Blackmail? Threatening your sister?" She was right. There was no point in sugarcoating the truth. He needed Gigi to remain vigilant about her safety. "And I'd hate to think what might happen once he gets what he wants from you. This isn't the kind of guy who'd leave a witness behind."

Her skin blanched. "I'll call Tammy and see if she can stay in Vegas for a couple more days."

"If she needs to come back for work, tell her to stay with a friend. She should be made aware of the situation. But it's easier to keep an eye on one of you than it is two."

Her fingers danced across the countertop to rest on the legal pad. "What do I do in the meantime? Besides solve the most important equation of my life."

He reached across the countertop to cover her hand with his, stopping the subtle drumming. He shouldn't make too much of this Gigi-whisperer superpower he'd discovered, but she seemed to center herself at his touch. When she turned her fingers into his palm, he had no problem holding on. "You pour me a cup of that coffee. You stay aware of your surroundings and know that I'll be close by."

Her lips softened with the hint of a smile before she pulled away to retrieve a mug from the cabinet. "I made myself a cup of tea. But I brewed coffee for Officer Cutler while she was here. I didn't know what you like to drink. Besides beer. I don't have any of that. Sorry."

He plucked a baby carrot from the plate she'd put in front of him and popped it into his mouth. "Technically, I'm on the clock, so I couldn't have a brewski, anyway."

"Do you want me to make you a sandwich?"

"Black coffee will do me just fine."

After setting a mug of the steaming brew in front of him, she set her tea in the microwave to warm it up before coming over to stand on the opposite side of the peninsula. "Sorry you got stuck with me. Again. You're a good sport to put up with my eccentricities."

He took a bite of one of the cookies, then paused a moment to savor the molasses, sugar and cinnamon before he polished it off and reached for another. "Good sport, nothin'. These are damn good." Her eyes widened at his, er, enthusiasm. "Sorry. I should have put that a better way. My mama, rest her soul, wasn't around long enough to teach me not to be a potty mouth. You made these?"

She hid a blush that warmed her creamy skin behind her mug and a long drink. "Mom was the knitter. I like to bake when I get stressed."

This woman could bake on top of being Einstein-level smart and all sorts of distracting? He'd never expected that heaven would wear horn-rimmed glasses, make him apologize for cursing and bake like his grandmother. Keir was right. He'd already lost a piece of his heart. "I've never regretted spending time with you, G."

The blush intensified before she turned away to clean the kitchen. Mixing bowls in the dishwasher. Wiping down countertops. Moving the plastic container stacked with cookies over to the peninsula where he sat. "Does that mean you're staying?"

"At least 'til I finish my coffee." Since reaching for Gigi to find out if her lips were as kissable as he remembered would be a monumental mistake in terms of professional ethics, he reached for the cookie container instead. "And a couple more of these. Or until you're ready to go to bed."

The beaters she was rinsing clattered into the sink. "Bed?"

"To sleep, G." That breathless gasp of anticipation stirred a response behind the zipper of his jeans. She'd made that same husky sound when he'd said something about heating up the bench on campus earlier that night. If he had a better read on women, he might think she was interested in him for more than protection or friendship. But he was probably just shocking her with the double entendre she read into his words. "You'll sleep inside," he reminded her, "and I'll be out in my truck."

"Of course. We could both use some rest before going into the lab." Her movements seemed jerky now, more hurried as she finished putting the kitchen to rights. "I'll be done in a few minutes. Then you can leave."

"I didn't mean..." Great. Now he'd hurt her feelings. "I'll stay as long as you want me to."

"No." She waved aside his apology without looking at him. "You have a job to do. You don't need to babysit me. The house is secure now, so I'll be fine. Brains and brawn, remember? You have bad guys to catch. I have numbers to decode—"

"G." He stood and circled around the peninsula. "Maybe we should talk about what's happening here."

"What's happening?" She stuffed the beaters into the dishwasher and closed the door. "Nothing's happening."

"How much experience do you have with men?" She groaned and walked away before he could reach her. "I think you might have a little crush on me, and it's making you nervous."

"I haven't had a crush on anyone since I was fourteen and graduating high school. I'm a grown woman now."

"I know it." He caught her hand and pulled her around to face him, hoping he could break this panicked embarrassment that made her flee from him. "Believe me, Ms. Legs, I know." At least she was listening to him now. Her gaze darted across his face, trying to read his expression. He rubbed the pad of his thumb across the back of her knuckles, telling her in every way he could that she could relax around him.

Her sensitivity or self-consciousness or whatever that outburst had been seemed to calm with every stroke. "Maybe I've got a little crush on you, too. I think we've got sort of a sexy professor/naughty student thing goin' on between us."

Her eyes narrowed with a quizzical frown. "That's a thing?"

"Yeah." He moved half a step closer. "I'd say it's definitely a thing."

Her fingers trembled beneath his. "Like Ian and his students?"

"No." Nothing like a reminder of the sexual-harassment accusations against her late boss to throw cold water on whatever was happening here. Hud stiffened and pulled away.

But her fingers turned to clench tightly around his. "Because you're a grown-up, too? And I don't have any power over you?"

Oh, she had some kind of power over him, all right. Maybe it was a fascination with someone who was so different from him. Or her social innocence—that seemed to trigger all kinds of alpha-male response in him with the urge to shield and support her. Or maybe it was the fact that she was just as isolated and too long without a meaningful relationship as he was that made him sense the kindred longing simmering between them. It made no sense how much he liked this woman, how much he wanted to protect her, how much he wanted to kiss her right now to see if that spark of attraction they'd felt two years ago had been a fluke—or if they hadn't given themselves enough of a chance to see what could happen between them.

Hud was reaching for the tendril of hair that had gotten caught behind the earpiece of her glasses when his phone dinged in his pocket. He muttered a curse when he heard another ding, indicating a long text. He let Gigi go to pull out his cell. *Next to no luck with the ladies.* He should get a T-shirt to commemorate his lousy timing.

"I'd better take this." She wasted no time in hugging her arms around her waist and retreating a step while Hud read the text messages from Keir. "We got one test result back from the lab. On your friend the security guard. Keir says there was enough Phenergan in his system to knock out a man twice his size."

"Poor Jerome."

Hud read aloud as he typed his response to Keir. "And Phenergan would be? How easy—"

"It's a superdose antihistamine," Gigi answered before he could finish the text. "It's also used as a sleep aid or treatment for nausea—especially travelers who are prone to motion sickness." Hud looked up at her, dumbfounded by the factoids cataloged inside that brain of hers. She shrugged. "Physics and engineering aren't the only sciences I've studied."

"Okay, Professor Smarty-Pants, do you know if that's an over-the-counter drug?"

"I'm pretty sure it's prescription only, Detective Lame-Nickname." He gave her credit for handing the teasing right back at him. "Is that important?"

Resilient wasn't a tough enough word to describe this woman's strength. "We can track any suspects who have access to that prescription." He typed the information to Keir and sent it.

"Will Jerome be okay?"

"The report from the hospital said he's resting comfortably. His wife is with him." He waited for Keir's thumbs-up emoji and then pocketed his phone. "Somebody definitely wanted him out of the way."

"Ian's killer?"

"Most likely." He shrugged on his jacket. Keir's text had been the reminder he needed to focus on the case, and not the redhead stuck in the middle of it. He wasn't the guy to teach Gigi about man-woman relationships, anyway. "I think we've done enough investigating for now. If we don't get a little shut-eye, neither one of us will be worth anything later today."

"Okay."

"Walk me out?" He took her hand, not wanting her to feel like he was leaving because of her. "I want to hear the dead bolt locking into place behind me." Some of the tension in him eased when she fell into step beside him. "Remember, you've got my number in your phone now. Call or text if you see or hear anything suspicious. Or if you remember anything you think might help the investigation." He didn't let go until they reached the front door. She unlocked it and pulled it open. The light from the porch lamp washed over them with an eerie yellow glow. He stepped outside but turned to reassure her. "Everything has been checked and rechecked. You're secure in your own home. I'll be out front, making sure everything's settled in the neighborhood. I'll drive you to the lab later this morning. You don't leave this house unless I'm with you. You don't let anybody in but me."

"Got it. Prisoner in my own home. Wait for you. Try not to be scared."

She rattled off the list by rote and Hud laughed. "I don't know when you're trying to be funny, or when you're dead serious. But you sure make me pay attention when you have something to say."

"Do you remember kissing me two years ago?" she asked out of the blue, surprising him as if she'd read the inappropriate thoughts on his mind earlier tonight.

No sense denying it. He trailed his gaze around the rectangle that framed her. "Right here in this doorway. Under this porch light. For a first kiss, I'm afraid I wasn't much of a gentleman."

"I've never forgotten it. Or you."

He swallowed hard at the earnest confession. Didn't that beat all? Had a woman ever said anything so good for his ego? But he'd paid the price far too many times for being the right man at the right time, and not the right man for the long term, to let the thrill of having made an impression on the brainy professor go to his head. He chuckled instead. "In a good way, I hope?"

Gigi looked stricken at the idea she might have insulted him. "Of course. You generated an exponential amount of body heat. You made me feel delicate and feminine. For a few seconds, I wasn't that weird, gangly kid surrounded by a bunch of grown-ups who knew more about life than I ever would. You kissed me like I was a woman. It was exciting and seductive and when I leaned into you, you didn't budge. That kind of strength is—" she lowered her chin and peeked over her glasses "—sexy." She whispered the last word as if they were sharing a secret—or that she'd never said the word to a man before. Hell's bells. Every muscle in his body tightened with that one husky word.

So much for not letting this woman go to his head. She played havoc with his good intentions. He wanted to take her in his arms and get this itch for her out of his system. "You thought all that while I was kissing you?"

"I'm always thinking. Except when I'm sleeping, of course. And even then, sometimes..." She adjusted her glasses on the bridge of her nose. No wonder she needed those little circuit-breaker touches to give her brain a rest. She was a whole new level of complicated he'd never dealt with in a woman. "I only wish I'd done a better job on my end. I wasn't very experienced. I'm still not—"

Hud pressed two fingers over her lips to silence her. "Easy, G. I'll have you know that I stewed over that kiss for a long time afterward, too."

Her eyes widened before she pulled back from his touch. "Because you felt guilty about giving in to social convention when you weren't really feeling it?"

Um, no. He didn't think he'd ever used the phrase *social convention*, much less worried about what anyone else might say when a woman was willing, and he wanted to kiss her. Gigi's emotional honesty required no less from him. "Because I wanted more. You were eager and hot, and it caught me off guard how much I wanted you. So, I backed off."

She dipped her hands into the pockets of her hoodie, looking all starchy and scientific as she considered his response.

"You thought I was hot?" Funny, what details registered with her.

Hud grinned. "You're not fishing for compliments, are you?"

She shook her head as though she had to move that notion aside to evaluate later. "Then why did you stop? I was into it. I was into you."

"I could tell. And believe me, that is all kinds of temptation to a man." He braced his forearm on the door frame beside her and leaned in, wanting to keep this conversation private from any curious neighbors. "I'm one of the good guys, though, remember? You said so yourself. I didn't want to take advantage of your situation that night. We'd just met, and it wasn't even a real date. And I could tell you're not a casual-fling kind of gal."

"I'm not. At least, I don't think I am. Although I've never had a fling. Or even really dated anyone seriously…" Her cheeks warmed with an adorable shade of pink. "I'm totally not cool admitting that, am I?"

"I hear enough lies in my line of work that your honesty is refreshing." He touched her hair, finally allowing himself the opportunity to relearn its smooth texture as he pulled that wayward strand away from her glasses. He studied its burgundy fire between his fingers before tucking it behind her ear and letting go. He stepped back, needing the late-night air to move between them to cool his skin and the impulses firing inside him. "They say that opposites attract, and yeah, I'm attracted to you. Something might have happened that night if you'd invited me in. But I didn't want you or me to have any regrets. Ultimately, you got to have

something in common to make a relationship work."
He pointed to her, then tapped his thumb against his
chest. "High society—working class. Brains—brawn.
Lady—potty mouth."

She mimicked his pointing, understanding his rea-
soning even if she struggled to make sense of the
desire she felt. "Outgoing—introvert. Experienced—
not." She retreated a step and hugged the edge of the
door. "So, we have no common ground on which to
base a relationship. And you didn't think I would go
for a one-night stand. That's why you ended the kiss.
That's why you didn't call."

"My gut said it was the right thing to do." Had she
missed the whole point of his not-having-anything-in-
common speech? "I'm the guy from the pool hall, G.
I don't get invited to fancy receptions at the Muehlebach like you do. The only letters after my name are
KCPD. I didn't think you'd say yes if I asked you out."

"For the record, I would have. I suppose if I'd been
more assertive, *I* could have called *you*. Tammy's always telling me to take charge and go after what I
want. I've just never applied that philosophy outside
the classroom or the lab." She offered him a rueful
smile. "And now we have Ian's murder to focus on.
What might have been, huh?"

"Yep. The opportunity was there, and we missed
it. Just my kind of luck." In two years, nothing had
changed. If he didn't walk away now, he never would.
"I promise, this missed chance between us won't affect my commitment to this investigation or to keeping you safe."

"I believe you."

Maybe there was hope of salvaging a friendship yet. "Good night, G."

He reached the edge of the porch before he felt a tug on the sleeve on his jacket. When he turned, Gigi's fingers slid along his jaw to pull his mouth to hers. Her soft lips molded to his, branding him with her surprising heat. Her kiss was sweet and chaste and brave for this woman, and Hud couldn't help but respond to her touch, to the fingers fisting in his jacket and scudding across the stubble of his beard to sink into his hair.

He settled his hands at her hips, sliding beneath her hoodie to find the slim nip of her waist. The tips of his fingers brushed against a strip of soft, warm skin between her top and pants, and the discovery triggered a satisfied growl in his throat. He held himself in check for as long as he could, savoring the tender, closemouthed kisses. Her arms drifted around his neck, her fingers clutching his scalp, tickling the nape of his neck, pulling herself closer until her long thighs butted against his. His arms moved with the same leisurely exploration around her waist until he palmed the smooth skin of her back with one hand and squeezed a handful of that decadent bottom with the other.

Gigi's sexy purr of frustration called to Hud like a siren. She wanted more and so did he. He lapped up her surrendering sigh and took over the kiss. He teased the seam of her mouth with his tongue, and when her lips parted, he drew her full bottom lip between his. He breathed in her warm vanilla scent and tasted the spice that lingered on her tongue when he thrust inside to claim her mouth.

He was good at noticing the details, too. Details were hot. Soft skin and silky hair beneath his fingers. The sweet taste of molasses cookies and eager woman against his mouth. The firm poke of a responsive breast beading against his chest as she pushed aside his jacket to get closer. Despite his best intentions, if Gigi wanted to make out on her front porch, then by damn, he was going to give the woman what she wanted.

They kissed and kissed, little pecks and longer drags, and Hud learned that slow and sweet was as heady as any fast-and-furious romp. The thickness pulsing behind his zipper wanted to take this lip-lock to a more private place where he could strip off these shapeless clothes and see just how far she wanted to take this kissing experiment. Her living room couch. Her bed. Hell, he could make do with the rug in the foyer so long as she wrapped those gorgeous legs around him and let him show her just how seriously mind-blowing this kind of chemistry lesson could be.

But, before his common sense could kick in and overrule his throbbing staff, Gigi pulled away. He hated to think that unsatisfied groan had come from his own throat. But since he doubted she'd ever initiated a kiss, he wasn't going to scare her away by demanding anything more.

Easing the tightness of his hold on her, he straightened her pajamas to cover her skin and rested his forehead against hers. Her glasses had fogged up to the point he couldn't see her eyes, so he studied her pink, swollen lips and the slightly abraded skin around her beautiful mouth. "Damn, woman. I'm not complaining, but what was that about?"

"Me going after what I want. In case I have to wait another two years for my next kiss." Her breath gusted through her nose. He was secretly pleased to discover she was struggling just as hard to get her breathing back to a normal rhythm as he was. He hadn't disappointed her. She sure as hell hadn't disappointed him. She studied her fingers as they smoothed the front of his shirts and straightened the collar of his jacket. Their busyness stopped and she tilted her gaze above her glasses to him. "You don't always have to be a good guy with me. Not if you don't want to be. I feel a connection, Hud. I wish you… I want you to…"

"To what?"

She curled her fingers into her palms and pulled away entirely. "I'll stop talking now. I've said more words to you tonight than I did to anyone else the entire week." She tugged off her glasses and pulled the hem of her T-shirt from under her hoodie to wipe them clean. "It's weird how I can talk to you. That doesn't usually happen outside work. I feel safe with you. I'm sure this is annoying. I have so many thoughts in my head, my words can't seem to keep up. Sometimes, it's easier just to shut up until I think of the right thing to say."

Uh-uh. She wasn't apologizing for wanting him. Or kissing him. Or admitting she was as much out of her depth with this attraction as he was. Hud tunneled his fingers into her hair, framing her face, moving in close enough for her to see him. "Don't you ever be afraid to say anything to me."

She evaluated him intently before smiling. "Thank you for not rolling your eyes when I explain things."

"Huh?"

"Trust me, it's a thing. Good night, Hud." She put her glasses back on and retreated into the house. "I'll see you in a few hours."

He inhaled a deep breath of autumn air. "Works for me."

He waited for her to lock the door before jabbing his fingers into his hair and facing the street. There wasn't a stitch of movement on the block. Parked cars. Dark houses. Was it paranoid to think this stretch of urban reclamation was too quiet? He climbed inside his truck and pulled out his cell to text his photos and observations to Keir at precinct headquarters.

Then he set his phone on the dash and leaned back against the headrest. Protection duty he could handle. But, hell. What was he supposed to do with that dump of information Gigi had just laid on him? She felt a connection. She wanted him to be a bad boy with her. She'd been thinking about kissing him for two years and couldn't wait a moment longer to kiss him again. She appreciated his strength and thought he was sexy.

There was nothing wrong with any of that. Especially when he felt a connection, too. His blood still simmered with the sweet fire of that kiss and the need in those curious, grabby hands. She was innocent and hot and his for the taking.

So why was he hesitating to embrace these feelings he had for her?

By the time he'd completed his next security sweep, he knew the answer.

He didn't want to get his heart broken again.

He didn't want to help Gigi discover the woman she

could be—the sexy, funny, smart, caring woman he already knew she was—and then lose her to another man. He didn't want to be the supportive friend, the safety net, and then be set aside when she no longer needed him.

He'd been lucky enough to awaken something in her, something stunted by the awkwardness of being a mental prodigy and her natural shyness. Like him, she'd become the parent to her younger sibling, putting Tammy's needs before her own while relationship opportunities passed her by. Now, Professor Virginia Brennan, Ph.D., was a free woman, established in her career. She was grown-up and aware of her desires. He was the nice guy she'd targeted for her attention.

But Hud didn't want to be the next scientific experiment in Gigi's life. The way she threw herself into a kiss, he had no doubt she'd be all kinds of amazing in the bedroom. And as complicated as her thought processes might be, he liked having a conversation with her. She didn't lie or put on airs. She made him laugh and baked like his Ozark grandma. But once she gained the confidence she needed to pursue a relationship, then what?

She'd leave *nice* and *safe* in the dust and find herself a man like Gary Haack or Ian Lombard, someone well educated and well-off, a man who she'd have a lot more in common with than a couple of passionate kisses.

# Chapter Eight

A loud bang from the neighbor's backyard jolted Hud's attention away from the update he'd been texting Keir. He saved the message to Draft and quietly slipped out of his truck. Gigi's front door was still locked, her windows closed, curtains drawn. Except for a dim glow seeping through the blinds of her bedroom window, she'd turned everything else off in the house and gone to bed. Some fine protector he was. What had he missed?

He tuned his ear to the creak of wood and panting breaths. Someone was running through the neighbor's backyard.

Wrapping his hand around the butt of his sidearm, Hud crossed the side yard to flatten himself against the gray siding. "KCPD!" he warned, hearing the crunch of footsteps in the leaves. "Step out and identify yourself."

"Izzy! Come back here." A quavering woman's voice shouted before a small dog popped around the corner of the house, dragging a leash behind it. The woman, wearing a gray tracksuit that matched the color of her hair, limped around the corner a moment after. Although Hud hadn't pulled his weapon, the older woman put her hands up. "Don't shoot. Stop her! Please!"

Hud stomped on the leash as the dog darted past him. After the sudden tug that flipped her over, the Pomeranian pounced to her feet with a high-pitched bark. But the moment Hud knelt and held out his fist for the dog to sniff, the puffball nuzzled his fingers. "Easy there, Tiger." After receiving a friendly lick, he scooped the dog up in one hand and handed her over to the woman. "Are you all right, ma'am? Are you hurt?"

"I bumped my hip on the deck railing when I tried to catch her. I'm too ornery to actually be hurt."

Relieved by the false alarm, Hud covered his gun and grinned at the reunion. "Is she an escape artist?"

"I'll say." The reprimand carried little weight as the woman hugged the dog to her chest. Then she extended an arthritic hand. "Kelly Allan. I'm Gigi's neighbor. This is Izzy."

Hud gently took her hand. "Detective Hudson Kramer."

"Usually, we don't go out for another hour, but something had her attention. She was scratching at the back door and shot out before I had a good hold on her leash."

"You heard something? Wait here." Instantly on guard, Hud pulled out his flashlight and moved around the woman to look through her backyard. A possum waddled along the back fence before disappearing beneath her utility shed. Birds chirped while nocturnal critters scuttled away before daybreak. Maybe he had nothing to worry about. The prowler who'd tried to break into Gigi's house hadn't returned.

Or maybe he had.

Hud hoisted himself up over the back fence to check the easement that ran behind the row of houses. Tire tracks. No leaves had gathered in them, so they had to be fairly fresh. He found them again in the mud behind Gigi's house. Still, there was no way to tell if the mud had been disturbed just a few minutes ago or late last night. He turned the flashlight and looked all the way up and down the empty gravel alley. Why did it feel like something sinister was surrounding Gigi Brennan? He was missing something important here but couldn't see it. Just in case, he snapped a picture of the tread marks with his phone. If he could match them up with a particular model of SUV tires, he'd update the BOLO on the car that had sideswiped Gigi's.

By the time he got back to the neighbor lady, neither she nor Izzy seemed alarmed by any sign of an intruder. He'd trust the dog on that one. "I don't see anything right now, ma'am. Looks like you've got a possum under your shed, though."

"That's Old Sam. As long as he eats the ticks and bugs in my yard, he can live there. Besides, he gives Izzy something to sniff around for." She squeezed her thin lips into a frown. "This was something else. Izzy doesn't pick up Old Sam's scent until she's out in the yard."

"Maybe your dog heard me," Hud suggested. "I

was doing a security sweep around Gigi's place a few minutes ago. Someone tried to break into the professor's house last night."

"I know."

Of course, she did. His gun and badge, and the squad car from earlier, would be hard to miss. He rested his fingers against the older woman's fragile elbow and escorted her to her back deck. "Then you know it might be safer if you wait until daylight to take Izzy for that walk."

Miss Allan's blue eyes sparkled with something other than moonlight as she smiled up at Hud. "Are you Gigi's new beau? Well, not that she had an old one, but are you?"

Had she seen that kiss on Gigi's front porch? When she winked at him, Hud knew that she had. While he appreciated that Gigi had a friend looking out for her, he also hated that his lack of willpower might stir what he suspected was a pretty healthy rumor mill at Gigi's expense. "I'm actually here to protect Professor Brennan. She's a witness to a crime I'm investigating."

The older woman stroked the dog's ears and winked. "I've never seen a police officer conduct an investigation like that."

Well, hell. Was he blushing? He doubted a sudden heatwave had blown through before dawn. "You don't miss a trick, do you."

"Not often. I know something's going on at the Brennan house. It's always quiet when Tammy's away. It hasn't been quiet tonight."

If Miss Allan had eyes on the neighbors, then she might be able to answer some questions. "Did you see anyone around Gigi's house earlier? Besides me and the uniformed officers, of course."

"I saw that man getting into his car. He nearly ran Gigi down."

Hud pulled out his notebook. "He was driving pretty fast, huh?"

"He wasn't driving. He got into the passenger side."

That could explain some of the discrepancies of the crimes surrounding Gigi. Having two perps, one impulsive, the other calculating; one unafraid of violence and the other with an aversion to it, explained a lot. "Could you describe the car that ran into Gigi's?"

"Black SUV, tinted windows. The man who got in was bigger than the driver, although I didn't see anyone's face. They wore stocking masks."

He jotted that down. "Are you sure?"

She tapped her cheek. "Cataract surgery. I've got good eyesight again."

No wonder she liked to spy on the neighborhood.

"You're proving to be a very helpful witness, Miss Allan."

"It's nice of you to say so." At Hud's insistence, she turned and carried Izzy up onto the deck. "I can tell by your accent and your manners that you're a Southern boy."

"As far south as Lake Taneycomo. Ozarks born and raised."

She paused when she reached the screen door. "What on earth would make you leave that beautiful part of the state and come up here?"

"My parents died. I was twenty years old and needed a job I could support my younger brother and sisters with. It was either the police or the military, and I wanted to be at home to keep my siblings together."

"Admirable. I dated a young man like you once. A Marine." Her sharp eyes dimmed, and she took on a wistful tone. "He was killed in Korea back in 1951."

"I'm sorry."

"I'm sorry, too. Ed was a good man. I would have married him if he'd come home to me." When she sniffed back her tears, Hud offered her the bandanna from his back pocket. "You're a good man, too. You take care of our Gigi, all right? I can tell she likes you."

"Yes, ma'am. I'll keep her safe."

She opened the door, but stopped, her sad expression abruptly changing. "And you should go ahead and have sex with her. I'm sure she'd like the idea if you asked—she might not think of it on her own. I swear sometimes that girl can't get out of her own head." She pushed the bandanna into his hand and squeezed his fingers. "It's those quiet ones you have to watch out for. Hidden passion. Every. Time."

Another heat wave washed over him. While he was a little embarrassed by the octogenarian's lack of a filter, he was also suddenly struck by the image of Gigi's long legs wrapped around his waist and her eyes darkening with desire while he explored every inch of that soft, creamy skin and buried himself inside her. Ah, hell. He seriously needed some sleep to dispel that fantasy. Or maybe he'd better just get back to work.

Miss Allan was safely on her side of the screen

door now. Hud backed away. "I will, um, take that advice under consideration."

He had a feeling Kelly Allan had been a handful long before she'd lost her Marine in the Korean Conflict. And she knew it, judging by the smile she gave him. "Aren't you going to ask me how I know she likes you?"

All right. He'd bite. "How? Because you saw her kiss me?"

"Because she invited you inside." She set the dog down and shooed it into the kitchen. "Other than workmen and Tammy's beaux, there hasn't been a man in that house since their father died." She latched the screen door. "Good night, Detective."

"Good night, ma'am."

The light came on in the front room of Kelly Allan's house, and Hud supposed she was watching to see if he was going to take her up on that sex-with-his-witness advice. He grinned and offered her a salute. He'd be out of a job if every citizen was as vigilantly aware of the world around them as Miss Allan was.

He turned his attention back to the soft glow of light through Gigi's window. He knew it was her bedroom from the security sweep he'd done inside the house earlier. He imagined her in bed with that legal pad, puzzling over the numbers in Ian Lombard's formula. He hoped exhaustion had claimed her, and she was finally getting the rest she needed.

Although he hated the circumstances, Hud liked watching over her. He knew it went back to his penchant for rescuing damsels in distress, for wanting someone to need him now that his younger brother and sisters no longer did. He liked knowing he could help, that she trusted him enough to ask for his help. He liked being close to Gigi, period. Nothing long-term was going to come of this bond forming between them. If he remembered that, maybe he could come out of this second-chance encounter with Gigi Brennan unscathed.

Settling in behind the wheel of his truck, he finished his report to Keir, adding Miss Allan's observations about the car and two intruders. As soon as he hit Send, his phone dinged with an incoming text alert.

He sat up straight when he saw Gigi's name. Had he missed something suspicious while he'd been chasing a possum and getting schooled on how to manage his love life?

His alarm eased into amusement. Kelly Allan wasn't the only woman who liked to spy out her window.

What did Miss Allan say to you?

Hud typed his response.

She could tell I was from the Ozarks. Said I remind her of an old boyfriend.

He hit Send and waited.

She didn't embarrass you, did she? She gives advice freely.

He absolutely would not mention the sex comment. Gigi had reached out to him again—invited him into her world, as the nosy neighbor had claimed. He hadn't been a part of anything but work for a long time. Even a text conversation with the auburn-haired professor made him feel the connection building between them.

She said there were two people in the car that hit you. I've got Keir tracking it.

Two people tried to break in?

Gigi appreciated knowing the facts, but he didn't want to scare her.

I'm not going anywhere.

Her reply was quick.

You don't have to sit in your truck all night.

Yeah, I do.

Why?

Was she worried about the intruders returning? Or asking why he cared enough to be here?
*She likes you,* Miss Allan had said.
Differences aside, impossible future notwithstanding, the feeling was mutual.

Because nobody gets to scare you, hurt you or make you feel unsafe in your own home. And I want to be first in line to ask you out for coffee when you wake up in the morning.

BREAKFAST QUALIFIED AS a date, right? Even drive-through coffee on the way to Williams University?

Gigi rolled onto her side and punched her pillow up to support her neck. She was going on twenty-four hours without sleep. She should be dead to the world right now. But between nightmares of Ian's pale lips gurgling up blood, and random numbers floating through her brain, trying to gel into equations, falling into a restful slumber had proved elusive.

Hudson was close by, keeping an eye on her home. While part of her relaxed in the security of his strong presence, another part of her hummed with anticipation. Hud wanted to take her out. She hadn't scared him off with that impulsive kiss or any one of her erudite ramblings and incidents of social klutziness.

Was this how Tammy felt when a man asked her out? Smiling so much her face hurt? Worried about what to wear, what to say? Anxious like a child about to embark on an amusement park ride, yet eager for the roller coaster to start?

She had no illusions about being easy for a man to want to spend time with. But she had hopes.

Hudson Kramer made her feel hopeful.

It might only be coffee. But to Gigi, it was everything.

She burrowed her cheek against the cool percale

and closed her eyes, savoring the unfamiliar anticipation, waiting for her alarm to go off at eight.

Next thing she knew, the alarm startled her from a deep, blank sleep.

She rolled onto her back, refusing to open her eyes against the morning sun that would be peeking in around the edges of her bedroom window. A moment later, she slit open one eye and frowned. Where was the sunlight? She glanced at the clock. Huh? She'd only been asleep for twenty minutes. That music wasn't from her alarm clock. It was her phone.

With a bam, bam, bam of surprise, awareness and worry, she pushed aside the covers and reached for her phone on the bedside table. She squinted a number she didn't recognize into focus and swiped the green arrow to answer the call.

"Hello?"

There were a dozen plausible explanations for a call before 7:00 a.m. on a Saturday morning. A wrong number. A concerned colleague who'd just heard about Ian's murder. Tammy finally getting her messages and calling from her Vegas hotel room to see if she was all right.

But Gigi listened to the measured, even breathing on the other end of the line and knew this call was none of those things. The anticipation that she'd fallen asleep to darkened with foreboding.

"Professor Brennan?" The breathing gave way to a hollow, mechanically distorted voice. Easy enough to achieve with a telephone app. There was no way to tell who was calling. "I want what Lombard gave you."

The note. An invisible fist tightened around her

heart and lungs. Gigi swung her legs off the side of the bed and turned on the lamp, scrambling to find her glasses. *Don't focus on the fear. Think, G. The police need you to find answers. You need to listen to this call.* "You already have it. You stole it out of my pocket."

"You know it's not the entire formula," the hollow voice continued. "I need the rest. I want you to get it for me."

This was Ian's killer. The man who'd attacked her. The man who'd stolen the information Ian had entrusted to her and who had tried to break into her home to steal the rest.

She needed Hud. KCPD could trace this number. He could touch her hand and dispel the fear that overwhelmed her. But she couldn't call for help or text him an SOS without ending this call. Searching for another idea, she pushed to her bare feet and hurried around the bed to the front window. She pulled open the curtains and snapped the window blind, sending it spinning around the top. Hud's truck was still parked in her driveway, just as he'd promised. But his chin was down to his chest, his face impossible to read in the predawn shadows. Was he hurt? Asleep? Looking down at his phone? Gigi knocked on her window, pressed her phone against the glass and pointed to it, willing him to look up and see her.

But he was too far away to hear, too engrossed in something else to see.

If he wouldn't come to her, then she needed to get to him.

"What if I say no?" she challenged, turning toward

the hallway. "You killed a man. I'm not going to reward you for that."

The hushed breathing was almost more unsettling than the cartoonish voice.

"Your choice." The hallway floor was cold beneath her feet as she ran to the front door. "I can make life very painful for you. I can end it entirely."

"End...?" She skidded to a stop. Her pulse thundered in her ears. Her breath came in quick, deep gasps. "Who is this? What do you want from me?"

"Don't play dumb, Virginia. It doesn't become you. I already killed Lombard for cheating me out of our bargain. I assume you'll be more cooperative."

His logic was flawed. "You won't kill me. You could have killed me at the lab, but you didn't. You need me alive."

"There are other ways I can hurt you. Ian's obsession with you was...misguided. I want to knock you down from your golden perch. Pluck every feather off you. Carve you into tender little fillets until you are screaming the information I need." The caller paused to let that image sink in, to let her understand that needing her and not harming her weren't mutually exclusive. "The same could happen to your sister, your boyfriend."

"My boyfriend?" Hud. He thought...? He'd been watching her closely enough that he'd seen the two of them together. Everyone who was important to her was in danger.

"Fail to cooperate and I'll kill them both and make you watch. You're good at watching the people you care about die."

Her skin crawled with the knowledge that this man had touched her things, touched her, while she'd been unconscious. But what he promised if she didn't do what he demanded was so much worse. "That's all I had of Ian's formula, I swear. I can't give you what I don't have."

A sharp knock drummed at her front door. Her startled gasp caught in her throat. He was here. The threat was here.

The voice droned on in her ear. "You know Ian's work better than anyone. You're the only one who can get me what I want. Their lives are on you."

"G! Are you all right? Open the door!"

Hud! He'd gotten her signal. Her toes seemed to stick to the floor when she tried to go to him. She stumbled, braced her hand against the wall to steady herself.

"Deliver Lombard's formula and the prototype to this address." While he rattled off an address in the industrial area off Front Street, she forced her stiff legs to move toward the door. "Write it down." She didn't need to. She wouldn't forget. Another curse of her complex mind. "Repeat it to me." She did. "I want that formula Monday morning at six."

The knock on her door became a pounding fist. "It's Hud. What the hell is going on?"

"What if I need more time?" She reached for the door. "That's less than forty-eight hours."

"This isn't a negotiation. And don't double-cross me like Lombard did. We'll be watching."

"We?" The slip of the tongue jarred her.

"Open the damn door or I'll break it down." A

heavy thump rammed the door, rattling the front of the house. Had he thrown his shoulder against it? "G!"

"I'm here." Her voice shook as badly as her fingers as she grabbed the knob on the dead bolt and turned it. The door swung open and Hud rushed inside, pushing her away from the opening and kicking it shut behind him. He held his gun down at his side. His chest expanded with a deep breath. His eyes—searching, intense—locked onto hers for a split second before he snatched the phone from her ear.

"This is KCPD. Identify…" She heard a click disconnecting the call before Hud even spoke. Hud looked at the phone, looked at her. "Talk to me right now."

Gigi hugged her arms around her middle. "He killed Ian. He said I was the only one who could… He wants me to… It took Ian years to develop those components and come up with workable designs, and I have forty-eight hours." She couldn't get warm again. She couldn't stop shaking. "He left me alive to…to finish Ian's work."

"Come here." Hud's arm snaked around her shoulders, pulling her to his chest. He holstered his weapon, stuffed her phone into his jacket and reset the dead bolt before wrapping both arms around her and sealing her against his abundant strength. "I got you."

She tucked her face against the juncture of his shoulder and neck and slid her arms beneath his jacket to anchor herself to his heat. He held her tight, his hand in her hair, his cheek rough against hers. He held her until she stopped shaking, until the rhythm of her breathing calmed and synced with his. She absorbed the scent of leather and the salt on his skin. She immersed herself in the healing power of being held, sheltered, surrounded by Hudson Kramer.

When she finally could release a breath that didn't burn through her chest, she eased her grip on him, although she was reluctant to pull away. His lips pressed against her forehead, and again at her temple. "I need to go to work, G," he whispered, before pressing a third kiss to her lips and unwinding himself from her arms. Hud shrugged off his jacket and had her slip her arms inside the sleeves before moving her away from the door. He nodded to the afghan draped over the back of the couch. "You want to sit and get warm? Or stay with me?"

She latched both her hands around his.

He nodded. With his hand firmly grasping hers, he led her through the house to check every lock on every door and window, ending up in her bedroom. He closed the blinds she'd opened to signal him and then pulled out his phone to call his partner and report on the situation. "I'm sure it's a burner phone, but track the number, just in case. And I want a record of every incoming call she gets here and at the university. I need a fresh set of eyes sittin' outside Professor Brennan's house, too," he told Keir. "We're runnin' on fumes here." Gigi pulled on a pair of socks while he talked, then straightened the quilt and sat on the edge of her bed while Hud and his partner made arrangements for tapping her phone and setting up round-the-clock coverage for her between Keir and his law-enforcement family. "Works for me." Hud glanced at Gigi and winked before answering his partner's question. "She's strong. She'll be fine." The fact that Hud believed that about her made Gigi believe it herself. She sat up a little straighter inside the leather jacket that engulfed her and nodded. "Shoot me a text. I'll be inside when you get here."

After he hung up, he pulled over a chair from her desk and set it down in front of her. He sat facing her, tugging her hands from inside the sleeves of his jacket to warm them between his in his lap. The calloused stroke of his hands around hers shot tendrils of heat through her skin and into her blood, sending his warmth throughout her body. "Good. They're not ice-cold anymore." His eyes that had glowed like a predatory wolf's when he'd first barged in to protect her had softened like a puppy dog's now that he knew she was safe and he'd taken steps to move his investigation forward. "I saw the lights going on, the blinds going up. It got my attention."

Every caress of his thumbs across the backs of her knuckles seemed to ease a little more of the tension inside her. "I couldn't think of how else I could without hanging up the phone. I tried to get to you. But then he said…"

"Tell me exactly what he said."

Gigi recounted everything from the heavy breathing to the less than forty-eight-hour deadline he'd given her to deliver Ian's work. She wasn't sure if it was intentional, but when Hud released her to write the information in his notebook, his knee shifted to touch hers, maintaining a constant contact she found both calming and intimate, like a secret shared between them. His knee remained there, warming a lucky spot of skin through denim and flannel as he copied down the address the caller had given her.

"There're nothing but warehouses and train tracks in that part of the city."

Hud tucked away his notepad. "We'll scout the location and set up a net to capture this perp when you make the drop. You won't be alone."

In the short time they'd been together, she was learning to read the nuances of Hud's expression. He didn't just mean Monday morning at the drop-off. He wouldn't be leaving her to face any of this on her own. Detective Brawn would keep her grounded, keep the fear at bay, so she could handle the brains part of this investigation. "After the staff meeting, I'll get on Ian's computer to see if I can locate the right file. I know a few places he'd hide things like a flash drive he didn't want anyone else to get their hands on."

"Maybe something there can tell us who he was meeting with last night. Or we can uncover if he's been doing nonuniversity business on the side."

Reluctantly, she pulled her knee away and leaned over to the bedside table to pick up the legal pad and study the equation. Her math was good. She'd already filled in some of the gaps and could project the outcome of the equation. But without knowing what result Ian was working toward, and how this breakthrough differed from the other research they'd been doing, she'd be making an educated guess. The application might not work with the minicapacitor's design if she didn't get it right. "What if I'm not smart enough to do this?"

Hud reached across the gap between them, gently

cupping her cheek and jaw. "I don't know anybody smarter than you."

While she appreciated the bolster of support, designing and building a working prototype would be challenging to complete in forty-eight hours, even under ideal circumstances. A dead mentor and the threat to hurt her or someone she loved were hardly ideal working conditions. "What if I can't figure it out before Monday?"

Hud dragged his hand down her arm to recapture her fingers. "It doesn't matter. They're not gettin' what they want. All we need is something plausible enough for them to take the bait. I'm not letting them get away with murder, assault, attempted burglary—and whatever else I decide to charge them with."

"He said he'll be watching me. Won't he know if I make something up? Also," she confessed, "I'm not very good at making stuff up."

Although he chuckled, the laughter never reached his eyes. "Juries love a clear motive. So yeah, it would be nice to have the formula and designs so we can clearly identify why your boss was killed. Especially if we can put a dollar value on what the killer wanted from him."

"And now me."

He plucked the legal pad from her lap and studied her math and drawings. Then he shook his head and set it back on the nightstand before reclaiming both her hands. "We're going to find out who these people are long before they get their prize, whether it's the real thing or a ruse."

"He…they…threatened to kill Tammy. And you.

And to…" She swallowed a hard knot of fear at the disturbing images the caller had described. "He sounded like he'd enjoy hurting me if I don't cooperate. Like he was hoping I would fight back. Just so he could—"

Hud swore before she could finish that sentence. "Get out of your head, G. Listen to me." Before she could read his intent, he'd scooped her up off the bed and pulled her onto his lap. His fingers feathered into her hair to tilt her head against his shoulder. Gigi grabbed a handful of his shirt and snuggled in as he anchored her between his arms and thighs. "I can take care of myself." His arms trembled around her, as if he was having a hard time stopping himself from squeezing her too tightly. "I'll have Keir put Tammy into protective custody when she gets into town. Nobody is going to hurt you. Not while I'm around."

"You're staying?"

"This bed looks like it sleeps two."

Gigi pushed away to look him in the eye. "You said we had nothing in common."

"You're afraid, and I don't like it. That's enough, isn't it?"

"That's not a logical syllogism."

"I don't know what that means. But I do know we both need sleep, even a couple hours of it, if we're going to solve this case and arrest these bastards." He stood with her in his arms, carrying her as if she was a dainty scrap of a woman, instead of someone who topped him by an inch or more. She felt the flex of his muscles, tightening to support her, then relaxing as he laid her gently on the bed. Perhaps she should be afraid of strength that could snap her like a dried-up

twig. But there was no fear with Hud—nervous anticipation, yes, but never fear. Despite fatigue and worry,
there was a thrill that quickened her pulse every time
he touched her. Parts of her seemed to heat up and
melt with every caress or kiss.

Hud's broad shoulders and stubbled jaw couldn't
be more masculine. She wondered…she wished…
Her poorly timed yawn confirmed that nothing other
than sleep was going to happen here over the next
hour. Just as well.

"You're good at taking care of people, Hud." She
shrugged out of his jacket, instantly missing the scent
and heat that had surrounded her. But when he sat
on the edge of the bed beside her, she didn't miss it
quite so much. "I remember when we played pool that
night, you said you'd raised your brother and sisters.
You gave up your home and moved to Kansas City so
they wouldn't be separated into foster homes. They
were lucky to have you. I'm lucky to have you, too.
For as long as you're willing to stay."

"I'm not going anywhere." He unhooked his belt
and set it, along with his gun and badge, on the nightstand beside her things. "Outside is too far away for
me to know you're safe—hell, the next room is too far
away—to know that that low-life coward isn't hurting you physically, or doing something to screw with
that big, beautiful brain of yours."

Gigi looked up into his rugged face, into his kind
eyes, and realized she'd never had a man carry her
to bed before, not since she was a little girl and she'd
fallen asleep studying or watching a movie, and her
father had carried her in. The essence of security was

similar, but there was little else that felt the same as Hud's promise to be here with her. These feelings of desire and trust were as overwhelming as they were unfamiliar. And yet, she couldn't imagine anything that felt more right, more inevitable than giving herself to Hudson Kramer.

But not now. Now, she needed something else from the man. She patted the quilt beside her. "Will you hold me?"

"Yeah. I'd like that." He sat in the chair to untie his boots, and then he was leaning over her. He removed her glasses and set them on the bedside table before pulling back the quilt. "Get under the covers. I'll sleep on top." Gigi scooted beneath the quilt, bracing herself as the mattress dipped with Hud's weight. He gathered her against his chest when she rolled over to face him and bring his handsome eyes and the dimple beside his mouth into focus. "This better?"

Nestling into the heat of his body, Gigi splayed her fingers over the reassuring beat of his heart. "Much. Is this okay for you?"

"Yes, Professor." He kissed her forehead, then nestled his chin at the crown of her hair. "Now go to sleep. We've got a whole hour before we have to get up."

Although desperate for a nap, her body hummed with a nervous energy. Her gaze shifted to the top button on his flannel shirt, and her fingers followed. The waffled material of his undershirt was soft, the buttons hard, the crisp curls of chest hair peeking through the veed neckline somewhere in between.

His skin leaped beneath the brush of her fingertips, like an electrical pulse had zapped from her touch.

He caught her hand against his chest, stilling her curious exploration. "Talk to me, G."

There had been an underlying train of thought she hadn't acknowledged. But now she did. "What if he calls again? He said he'd be watching me, so I can't cheat him out of what he wants."

His right hand traced leisurely circles against her back. "From here on out, you don't answer your phone without me listening in. He's not going to terrorize you anymore. I want him to deal with me."

"Won't that just make him angry?"

"He doesn't know angry until he sees me pissed off." Even in that lazy drawl of his, even in that hushed tone, she heard the vehemence of his promise. "That's what will happen if he threatens you again."

Emotions swelled inside Gigi that logic couldn't process, and shyness and self-preservation could no longer contain. She pushed herself up on her elbow and pulled his mouth up to hers in an impulsive kiss.

She knew something better than satisfaction when his hand cupped the back of her head and his lips moved against hers. She was aware of her breasts pillowing against his chest, his hand settling at the curve of her hip, that husky growl rumbling in his throat, and far too many barriers of covers and clothing between them before she pulled away.

She rode the rise and fall of his chest before he tucked her back against his side. "Not that I'm complaining, but what was that for?"

"I don't always express what I'm thinking and feeling in a way that others understand. But that way seems to work for you and me."

"I think I get the message, Professor." She felt him smile against her forehead before he kissed her there. "You're welcome."

## Chapter Nine

By noon on Saturday, Hud realized he was well and truly screwed in the self-preservation department.

Now that the CSIs had cleared the scene at Williams University, Hud stood in the doorway to Ian Lombard's office, watching a team of graduate students clean up the lab and inventory what the KCPD criminologists had left behind, while Gigi sat at her late boss's desk, searching through his computer for any leads on Lombard's unfinished formula. Thanks to the glass windows in each of the offices, he could monitor all the activity in the technology lab from this vantage point.

Keir sat in Evgeni Zajac's office with Hana Nowak and an international-law attorney from the Lukinburg embassy, trying his hand at getting the visiting professor to share his insights about the victim and his alibi for the time of Lombard's murder. The old grouch had plenty of accusations about Ian Lombard—from hogging the spotlight at last night's reception to hitting on his raven-haired wife—but no real leads beyond admitting he'd argued with Lombard at the reception about whose name should be at the top of the paper they were presenting back in Lukinburg. Since they'd worked as a team to develop the capacitor design, in his home country where he was a revered scholar, his status should be reflected in the presentation. Was a coworker he believed had taken credit for what was rightfully his enough motive for murder?

As for Zajac's alibi? His wife corroborated his claim that they'd left the reception and were driving home when they'd gotten the call about Lombard's death and had headed to the university instead. Beyond that, Hana Nowak wasn't saying much. She wore dark glasses, complained of a headache and was letting the attorney do most of the translating for her husband.

Although Keir had peeked behind Hana's glasses and said he'd seen no signs of abuse or even the tears she'd been crying last night, Hud had already moved Dr. White Hair to the top of his suspect list. He'd caught Gigi wincing when she'd slung her backpack over her shoulder that morning. She'd dismissed his concern that she was feeling an aftereffect from her assault, but, with a little prodding, had reluctantly shown him the bruises Zajac had left on her arm at the reception.

Hud had wanted to arrest the man then and there, but Gigi and Keir both had reminded him of the bigger prize they were after—Lombard's killer. A man with that big of an ego, that much of a temper, was the kind of man who'd get into a fight with a rival, trash a lab and stab his opponent with the most convenient weapon available. But would Zajac have the patience and forethought to drug a security guard?

Zajac wasn't the only research team member who didn't seem to see Lombard's death as a loss. The day after his boss's murder, everything was business as usual for Gary Haack. The bearded blond man had shown up for the eleven o'clock emergency staff meeting with the dean and department chair in his neatly pressed suit and tie, and had taken charge of cleaning up the lab.

He'd tried to take charge of the meeting before that, too, interrupting Gigi's response to a question about Lombard's current workload. Haack strode to the front of the table and draped his arm around Gigi's shoulders in a show of solidarity, giving an eloquent speech about staying the course and carrying on their research because huge discoveries were within their grasp. Gigi had visibly squirmed.

Hud had been ready to march across the room, break Haack's arm and remind the self-important stooge that Gigi was the one who'd called the dean to set up this meeting. But even as Hud acknowledged Keir's warning nudge to suppress his instinct to rescue her, Gigi touched her glasses and scooted away from the tall man's grasp. She circled around the conference table, burying her hands deep in the pockets of her white lab coat. He suspected those hidden hands were twirling a pen or shredding a tissue, but outwardly, she was calm, well-spoken, professional. Today was about supporting each other, she'd said. Making sure the entire faculty, staff and student body felt safe at Williams. She thanked the dean for making counselors from the student health department available to anyone who needed to talk. Today was about rebuilding the sanctity of the lab and remembering the good things they could about Ian Lombard. The dean and a few of the staff shared stories about Lombard's impact on their lives. Hud recognized the tactic for what it was. She didn't necessarily want to be in the spotlight, but she was still controlling the meeting.

When Gigi had looked to him, he'd winked and grinned with pride. Who understood interpersonal relationships now, Haack?

Now with his stomach rumbling for the lunch they'd missed, Hud crossed his arms over his chest and leaned against the doorjamb. Could there be anyone else with a motive to kill Lombard beyond these people here? The first forty-eight hours of an investigation were all about finding leads and closing in on a definitive suspect so KCPD could wrap up the case before the press tainted the facts and the perp had time to go underground and disappear. He and Keir had plenty of suspects and motives, but almost twenty-four hours in and they weren't anywhere close to making an arrest. And, with the threats to Gigi, the perp was the one calling the shots.

Could the killer really be someone this close to her?

While Zajac circled the wagons to protect himself and his wife from any sort of accusation, Haack had asserted his authority by supervising the grad students in the lab. Every now and then Haack's gaze darted over to Gigi, perhaps curious about what she was looking for in Lombard's office—or maybe worrying that she was stepping into Lombard's position. He somehow doubted that Haack would accept Gigi's authority over him.

Maybe he should move Haack ahead of Zajac on his suspect list.

Hud's fingers itched in a closed fist as he recalled the tall man's proprietary claim on Gigi, when clearly, whatever he thought was happening between them wasn't mutual. Maybe Haack's interest in Gigi had more to do with control than attraction. If Gary couldn't get ahead of her academically and professionally, then he'd undermine her personally—keep her stuck in her shy shell, make her dependent on him. Hud didn't have a good read on the engineering professor yet, other than the smell of money and a long streak of entitlement running through his veins. Hud's instincts said Haack was a man with a hidden agenda. Now whether that agenda was to take over Lombard's research project, world domination or simply getting into Gigi's pants, Hud didn't know. But he didn't trust the guy.

Still, Lombard's unsolved murder wasn't what had him in such a mood this afternoon. Hud could credit his restless impatience with this murder investigation with the nearsighted redhead in the office behind him.

He'd slept aroused for an hour while Gigi snored softly in his arms. The woman liked to touch and explore with her hands, but that was nothing compared to the way she snuggled up against him, demanding every inch of body-to-body contact he could give with layers of clothing and a fluffy quilt between them. He wondered if she'd been as painfully aware as he was of how her thigh had wedged between his legs, unconsciously cupping his groin and making him wish there weren't ten layers of cloth between them, ensuring that he couldn't get to Gigi's body, no matter how badly that most male part of his anatomy wanted to. Maybe she spent so much time inside her head that her body felt neglected, or maybe she'd never had the opportunity to explore and embrace the differences between her soft, lithe body and a harder son-of-a-gun like him before. Maybe she'd been so afraid, so alone, that the only way she could relax enough to sleep was to feel him pressed tightly against her, surrounding her, promising to keep the unseen enemy at bay.

His emotional survival had gone right out the window when he saw that frightened look on Gigi's face as she held the phone to her ear, a look put there by whatever vile things that pervert had said to her. Good luck. Bad luck. No luck with women. It didn't matter. Gigi had wormed her way inside his head and his heart. Walking away from her before he got burned was no longer an option. She needed him. Yeah, she needed the kind of protection a cop could provide. But he couldn't stand back and let any other man or woman with a badge take the lead on this case.

Gigi Brennan needed *him*. To touch her. To hold her. To hear the pleas for help and insightful revelations mixed up with all her big words and awkward ramblings. She needed him to help her feel safe enough to explore her desires and understand her feelings.

And he needed her to… Hell. He needed her to need him, to see him as her hero, to want him for the man he was. He'd had two whole years and half a weekend to decide that his feelings for Gigi were real.

It might not last. She might wake up one day and realize that he wasn't the only man ogling those gorgeous legs, or who appreciated that sexy intelligence and was charmed by her shy vulnerability. For now, for the duration of this investigation—until the killers were caught and the threat to her had ended—Hud was in this relationship. They'd missed their chance to connect two years ago. And most of the impediments that could keep the two of them from lasting as a couple were still there.

But for forty-eight hours, at least, this woman had his heart. She'd have his gun and his badge—and his life—if she needed it.

After Monday morning, the need would be gone. Reality would creep in and push them apart. A killer would be behind bars, he hoped, she'd feel safe and he'd be sent back into the friend zone, relegated to sidekick status again. After this case was closed, it would be up to Gigi to decide if they had any chance at a future. With his luck—

"Hud?"

Thank God he didn't have to finish that thought.

Turning from his observation position, he frowned at the shadows that looked like bruises under her eyes. She'd been working too long at this, but with the time crunch hanging over her head, he doubted he could convince her to take a break. Instead, he circled the desk to look over her shoulder at the computer screen. He saw rows and rows of numbers with dates and time stamps. A log of some kind. "What did you find?"

"Nothing about the formula. But I did find this."

"What am I looking at?"

This morning, she'd twisted her hair up into a bun at the back of her head after putting on black pants and a blouse to come to the lab. She pulled out a pen she'd tucked beneath her hair clip and used it to point out items on the screen. "These are our power-consumption records. Because of heightened security and the sensitive nature of some of the compounds and equipment we work with, the lab is on its own power grid. When we're all here working, of course, we need more power. But when we're gone for the night, the lab is on a cycle that reduces power. There's enough to maintain the security locks and protect ongoing experiments."

"You said the power was out when you found Lombard. The guard had to reboot the system."

Gigi nodded and pointed to line number twenty-seven. "Someone accessed the power grid Thursday night to alter the consumption cycle."

Hud gripped the back of her chair, not yet understanding the point she was making. "Lombard was killed Friday night."

She scrolled down the page and pointed to nine o'clock Friday night. "Somebody programmed the blackout. Right from this computer. A complete system shutdown. I got here about ten p.m. Jerome was already asleep at his desk."

Hud straightened. "The blackout would take lab security off-line?"

She nodded. "Any entries or exits from the lab couldn't be tracked. No key cards or codes would be recorded. No cameras would be working. Whoever Ian was meeting wouldn't show up in any records."

"His killer could have been lying in wait for him. With the lab dark, he'd never see the attack coming.

Maybe the plan was to lure your boss into a trap and force him to give them the formula."

"I have one question."

"Only one?" He had nothing but questions. A couple of concrete answers would go a long way toward solving this murder and ending the threats against Gigi.

"Why would Ian come into the lab if the power was off?" She logged out and shut down the computer. "This place was his baby. If he thought something was wrong, he'd have called the campus police. He'd have turned the power back on himself to protect his work."

Hud had an idea about that, although he wasn't sure Gigi would like it. "You said your boss was a player. If the right temptation came along, promised something he couldn't resist, mightn't he set up a clandestine rendezvous that couldn't be traced? That wouldn't get back to his wife?"

She surveyed the room, her gaze finally landing on the whiskey bottle and glasses still sitting on their tray on the coffee table in front of the couch. "That would explain the two glasses. He was coming here to meet a woman. He left me at the reception to deal with Evgeni while he…" Her breath seeped out on a disappointed sigh. "Ian left a note for Jerome saying he had a meeting and didn't want to be disturbed. Then he powered down the lab to hide his comings and goings and enjoyed a drink and an argument that got way out of hand. But how does date night gone bad have anything to do with the formula? And who doctored Jerome's coffee?"

He moved his hand to squeeze her shoulder. "The

woman set him up. Preyed on his weakness. Promised him a few favors in exchange for a look at his work. We think she had a partner, so it could have been an elaborate setup to force your boss to turn over his formula." Gigi's gaze followed his when he looked through the windows to the other people moving throughout the lab and faculty offices. "Any candidates out there for our mystery woman?"

"He liked them blonde and curvy." Her voice was barely a whisper. "One of the grad students?"

"Does it have to be a blonde?" He spotted Zajac and his wife leaving the lab while Keir finished up a conversation with their attorney. "Hana Nowak seemed genuinely upset about Ian's death."

"If they were having an affair, I didn't know about it. Of course, I don't pick up on those kinds of cues between people. But if Evgeni found out, that could explain his temper lately." Gigi shook her head. "For the brains of this operation, I'm not being very helpful, am I. I can't find any notes about the new capacitor design anywhere. Encrypted or not, if Ian was hiding the formula here, it's gone."

"The killer wouldn't still be coming after you if he had it."

"Still doesn't make me feel very useful. Can I get out of here now?" Although the crime lab had taken the rug where Ian Lombard had bled out and died, along with several other items, there were still plenty of memories in this room to haunt Gigi. "I need to take a break."

"You're doin' great, G." Hud pulled her to her feet.

"Just a few more things we need to wrap up here. Then I'll treat you to an early dinner."

"Our second date." All the reasons why they couldn't have a lasting relationship faded into little blips of white noise when she smiled at him like that.

But the moment they stepped out of Lombard's office, Gary Haack was there, blocking Gigi's path. "Do you have a minute?"

Hud slipped his hand to the small of Gigi's back and pulled her to one side. "No, she doesn't."

Gary shifted to stop them from crossing the lab, holding his hands up in surrender. His apologetic smile looked friendly enough, but Hud didn't trust it. "Look, Detective, I know you and I got off on the wrong foot. I didn't realize the two of you were an item when I tried to step in and help last night. I guess it wasn't meant to be."

"Gary… We work well together. Why can't you be satisfied—"

He cut off Gigi's protest before it could gather any steam. "On paper, you and I would make an unstoppable team. Like Pierre and Marie Curie or the Mosers. But I see now you want something different. I know when to make a graceful retreat."

Like hell he did. What game was he playing now?

"Different?" Gigi echoed, turning to Hud. "I'm a normal…" She tilted her gaze up to Haack. "How is what I want different…?"

"You got a point, Stringbean?" Hud prodded. He understood the snide put-down in Haack's surrender speech was meant for him, even if Gigi didn't.

"Wow. I haven't heard that one since high school,"

the taller man deadpanned. "Did you come up with that all by yourself?"

"Would you two stop," Gigi chided. "I'm helping the police with their investigation. What's the issue? Can it wait?"

"Not if we want to get this inventory done before your friends leave." Gary smoothed the lapels of his spotless white lab coat as he included Hud in his answer. "It's a lab question that has nothing to do with your case, Detective. It will only take a couple of minutes."

If Hud didn't need that inventory to determine what, if anything, had been taken from the lab, he'd have shuffled Gigi as far away from Professor Fancy Pants as he could. But that was his personal aversion to the man talking. He and Keir *did* need the inventory for potential evidence. Plus, he wasn't about to undermine Gigi's authority here. If she was the expert Haack needed to consult, then she needed to do her job. Hud met Haack's arrogant gaze straight on as he removed his hand from Gigi's back. "Go do your thing, G. I'll wait for you in your office."

"The VPAL needs to be repaired. But we also talked about replacing it at our last budget meeting. If you'd give me your two cents…"

Haack cupped Gigi's elbow and the two professors walked over to inspect a piece of machinery. Hud's fingers curled into a fist down at his side. "I'd like to give him my two cents."

Keir ended his conversation with the Zajacs' attorney and joined Hud, nodding down at the fist beside his thigh. "Not getting along with the locals?"

Hud flexed his fingers, forcing them to relax. "Can I make a guy a suspect because he's a smug bastard who's playin' G for a reason I haven't figured out yet?"

"Well, it won't hold up in court, but I understand."

His partner's comment diverted Hud's attention. Of course, Keir would understand this deep-seated suspicion and worry. He'd met his wife shortly after she'd been brutally assaulted. Back then, every man his wife knew had been a suspect in Keir's book. Plain and simple, personal feelings complicated an investigation.

Gigi rejoined them as the two men traded a fist bump, and the three of them went into her office. "Did you two uncover something to celebrate?"

It was impossible to explain the bond two long-time partners like he and Keir shared. "Nah. We're just a couple of bros who are preternaturally joined at the hip."

An eyebrow arched above her glasses. "Preternaturally?"

"Despite what Haack says, I know what a few big words mean."

"I wasn't implying that you didn't," she answered, upset that she might have insulted him.

"No worries, G." He cupped the side of her jaw and made sure she saw the humor in his eyes. "I'm teasing. Your friend Haack puts me in a mood."

"He puts me in a mood, too." She reached up to rub her hand up and down his forearm before breaking contact to pull her backpack out of her desk. "That interruption was just him getting me alone for a few minutes. He wants me to support his application to head up the research team now that Ian's gone. He said he's more leadership material than I am—that I'm a good worker bee he wants to keep on the team."

"Worker bee? He said that?" Hud followed her while Keir closed the door for privacy. "I hope you told him to stuff it. You ran that meeting this morning like you owned the place."

"I was a nervous wreck."

"It didn't show. You handled it because you had to do it."

He saw the brief flash of a smile before she shrugged out of her lab coat. "Thanks. I told him I didn't want to talk to the department chair about that yet. We haven't even had Ian's funeral. And with this forty-eight-hour deadline hanging over my head…" She shook her head as she pulled out the ivory sweater she'd washed last night. She fingered one of the stains that had faded to a blush pink. That had been Lombard's blood, and whatever comfort the hand-knitted garment had given her in the past was gone now. Instead of putting it on, she stuffed it inside her backpack. "I can't even think about what happens beyond Monday morning."

Hud pulled his leather jacket off the back of her chair and draped it around her shoulders, squeezing her upper arms to remind her there were other places she could find the solace she craved. "Deep breaths, G. We'll get through this one day at a time—one minute at a time if we have to."

Keir joined them on the opposite side of the desk, keeping them on task. "Did you check your office?"

Gigi nodded, stepping away from Hud's grasp to sink into her chair and open the top drawers to reveal the mess inside. "Someone's been through it. Things are out of place. Just like my backpack and billfold were. Your lab people dusted for prints but didn't find any but mine."

"Just like everywhere else. Whoever was here wore gloves. Anything missing?" Hud asked.

She shook her head. "It's creepy to know that someone has touched all my stuff, maybe even while I was on the floor, unconscious."

Gigi's obvious discomfort doubled Hud's desire to get her out of here. But there was still work to do before they could take the break she desperately needed. He turned to his partner. "Did you complete the background check on Haack? We know he comes from old money. Please tell me he got disinherited or has a gambling or drug issue."

"Sorry. His financials look solid. If he's hurting for money, there's no record of it."

Gigi slid her arms inside the sleeves of his jacket and hugged it around herself. "Gary might kill Ian out of jealousy, but why threaten me to produce the rest of Ian's formula? We could just work on it together at the lab."

"Who'd get credit for the invention?" Hud asked. "Whose name would be on the patent?"

"Both of ours. And I'd insist on including Ian, since he developed the idea first."

Keir shared Hud's bad vibe on Gary Haack. "A man with his ego might not want to share the glory."

Hud agreed. "And if he's working with a partner, as we suspect, the partner could be the one who needs the money from the sale."

Keir had another idea. "The partner could be holding something over his head, too. Forcing him to be the accomplice."

"*If* Gary's the one behind this," Gigi clarified. "He could just be a class A jerk."

"That's a given." Hud conceded his theories were all speculation thus far. "Guess I can't arrest a man because I don't like him putting his hands all over you."

Soft gray eyes shot up to meet his gaze. "Teasing?"

"No."

A blush colored her pale cheeks as she quickly ducked her head and went back to straightening her desk. Yep. *Smooth move, Kramer.* That had just come out as possessively caveman as it sounded. He glanced over to see Keir's amused look that said he knew just how far and how fast he'd fallen for Gigi.

Determined to stave off another lecture on the ill-advised impulses of his love life, Hud turned their focus back to the investigation. "Your blackmailer has to be someone with access to you here. Besides Haack, we've got Zajac." He turned to Keir. "What did you find out from him?"

"Directly? Not much. Either he thinks we're suspicious of him, or he's truly hiding something." With a wink that told Hud he understood the diversion for what it was, Keir pulled his cell phone from his jacket and scrolled through his texts. "I reached out to Carly Petrovic." Carly was a former undercover officer Hud and Keir had provided backup for on a couple of cases. On one of her assignments, she'd helped protect a bona fide prince, and now she was married to the manager of IT security at the Lukinburg embassy.

"Her husband put out some feelers for us. He says there's chatter about some Lukin dissidents—a new mob descended from the previous regime—who are trying to reassert their power. The dissidents are trying to arm themselves to carry out a terrorist attack. A couple of their suspects have applied for visas to come into the US."

Gigi stood beside Hud. "Homeland Security won't let them into the country, will they?"

Keir shrugged. "Captain Hendricks is notifying local and state authorities. If the Lukin government doesn't lose track of them, and they aren't traveling under false documents, we should be able to prevent them from coming to Kansas City."

Hud had a lot of experience reading his partner's expressions. And the one he wore now didn't inspire him with confidence. "But the Lukins have already lost track of their suspects, haven't they?"

Keir nodded and typed in a text. "They're off-the-grid. Carly and her husband are doing everything they can to track them down, whether they're still in Europe or here in the States. I can find out if one of them is a blonde."

Hud felt the brush of Gigi's fingers against the back of his hand. He would never deny her when she was brave enough to reach out to him, and quickly linked his fingers with hers. "Could Dr. Zajac and his wife have a connection with the Lukin dissidents?"

Keir eyed the clasp of their hands. "The professor adamantly denies supporting anyone from the old Lukin regime. The new government gave him freedom to pursue his own research, and he's grateful for the opportunity. That's about all his attorney would let him say."

"What about Hana? She has connections to Lukinburg, too. Could she be working with the dissidents?"

"She didn't say much. Kept complaining about her headache. Said she hasn't felt well since stepping off the elevator. Motion sickness, I guess. I imagine being married to that blowhard doesn't help." Keir swiped aside his texting and punched in a number. "I'll ask Carly's husband to dig a little deeper into Hana's background, see what he can find out."

Keir put the phone to his ear and left just as Gigi's phone chimed from the pocket of her backpack.

Her hand went cold within his grasp. "Do I have to answer it? What if it's him?"

The hollow voice that had threatened everything she cared about.

Hud pulled her phone from its pocket and set it on the desk without releasing her hand. Pulling out his own phone, he punched in a number to request a trace on the incoming call. "Put it on speakerphone. I'll be right here."

Nodding, Gigi answered the call. Her voice was quiet, cautious. "Hello?"

"Virginia?" a woman's voice answered in a clear, unaltered tone. "Is that you?"

"Yes?"

The noise in the background—indistinct conversations, a loudspeaker, traffic noises—indicated the woman was calling from a public place. "Oh, thank goodness I reached you. This is Doris Lombard."

"Doris?" Gigi's tone lost that breathy suspicion and

she released Hud's hand as compassion overrode her fear. False alarm. Hud deleted the text and tucked his phone back into his pocket. "Sorry, I was expecting someone else. How are you holding up? Are you on your way back to Kansas City?"

"I'm here. At the airport." The roar of a plane taking off in the distance confirmed her location. "Is there any way you can come pick me up? Ian dropped me off back in July, so I don't have my car. And I've been too upset by everything that I forgot to hire a car. It's rush hour and it'll take forever to catch a cab home. Would you mind? I've been surrounded by strangers for hours. I'd appreciate seeing a friendly face."

Gigi shook her head before she answered. "Oh, Doris. I'm so sorry. I can't. My car is in the shop. I had..." She glanced over at Hud, searching for the words to downplay everything that had happened for the grieving widow. "I had an accident."

"Oh, my goodness. Are you all right?"

"I'm fine. I'll be fine." She energized her tone again. "You're the one I'm worried about. I was there when Ian died. I tried to save him. I'm so sorry I couldn't."

"Don't you worry about that. I'm glad he had a friend with him at the end. That means a lot to me." They heard the warning siren of a luggage carousel about to turn on. "Is there another time when you and I can talk? I was making plans on the flight, and I was thinking—if you'd be willing... Not everyone was a fan of Ian's—would you give the eulogy at Ian's service? I know he'd love it if his prize protégé said something kind about him."

"Eulogy? In front of everyone?" Hud watched the color draining from Gigi's face and pulled out the chair for her to sit down. "Will it be a big service?"

"I imagine. Colleagues from the university. Students. Of course, family and friends." Hud sensed the numbers growing exponentially in Gigi's head and squeezed her shoulder to stop her from imagining the worst. "We'll talk about it soon. All right?"

"All right. Soon. Again, I'm so sorry about the ride. Do you want me to ask someone else to pick you up?"

"No. I'll suck it up and deal with the cab line. I just thought we could kill two birds with one stone. I'll call you later. Goodbye, Virginia."

"Bye."

Gigi stared at her phone for several seconds after ending the call. While this hadn't quite escalated into a panic attack, Hud needed her to do him and KCPD a big favor. He knelt beside her, gently brushing aside a lock of fiery hair. "My truck is parked right out front."

She knew exactly what he was asking and shook her head. "I don't want to talk about Ian's funeral. I don't know how to help her with her grief. And I really don't want to stand up in front of a huge crowd and deliver a eulogy."

"You could do it if you had to, G. From what I've seen, you can do anything you put your mind to. But right now, I need you to call her back. We *want* to drive Mrs. Lombard home."

"We do?"

"You're not finding anything here. The next logical place where Lombard might hide something is at his house." He glanced through the windows into the lab to see Gary Haack quickly adjusting his glasses and turning away from spying on them. "Besides, I wouldn't mind puttin' a little extra distance between you and these suspects."

Gigi swiveled her chair toward Hud, searching for something in his eyes. "You think Doris would let us look around?"

He rose to press a soft kiss to her lips. He'd meant to encourage her, but her fingers settled against his jaw, and her tender, eager response soothed a raw spot inside him before he pulled away. "I know it's asking you to step out of your comfort zone, but I need you to ask her."

His lips tingled as she trailed her fingertips across the line of his mouth. Then, she lifted her shoulders and turned back to the desk. "I'll call her back, tell her we're on our way."

## Chapter Ten

Gigi climbed down from the back seat of Hud's truck while he retrieved Doris Lombard's rolling carry-on bag. She would have waited to climb the pillared front porch with him, but the older blonde woman linked her arm through Gigi's and pulled her into step beside her to enter the stately white home.

Although there were clearly staff or at least a regular cleaning crew taking care of the two-story Colonial, based on its home-magazine-worthy decor and dust-free surfaces, there was no one here to welcome the mistress of the house. Doris had shed tears on the drive from the airport and shared her plans for her husband's service once the medical examiner's office released Ian's body from the lab. But as soon as she pushed open the front door, Doris heaved a relaxing breath and smiled.

She led them into a study where bookshelves framed a painted brick fireplace. "You can toss your jackets here."

Doris unbuttoned the jacket of her taupe suit and laid it across the back of the first of two black leather sofas. Gigi had been to the home a couple of times before and recognized this room as Ian's home office. Anticipation buzzed thought her veins. This would be the spot to find something that could help her crack the meaning behind Ian's cryptic notes. "Can I get you anything?" Doris asked, heading to the liquor cabinet behind the desk.

"No, thank you." Gigi shivered inside Hud's leather jacket, while he'd pulled a black KCPD windbreaker to put on from the back of his truck. But Doris seemed unaffected by the autumn chill in the air. Maybe she'd adapted to the cooler temperatures in Scandinavia, and a brisk evening in Missouri felt balmy by comparison. "How was the weather over in Norway?" she asked. Maybe she was the only one sensitive to the cooler temps. Or maybe her curious mind couldn't help but get distracted by things that didn't seem to fit. "Is it cold there?"

"Very. They get their winter much sooner than we do here."

"And yet you have no coat." Gigi eyed the sleek silver carry-on as Hud set it down and joined them in the study. The small suitcase was the only luggage they'd retrieved from the airport. "I doubt anything substantial would fit into your bag."

"Gracious." Doris looked down at her silk blouse and skirt. "I must have left it on the plane. I was so upset about Ian, I just wanted to get home," Her eyes crinkled up and she sniffled.

Gigi was no good at understanding people's emotions. She'd let a potential puzzle get in the way of her compassion. She quickly pulled out a tissue for the other woman. "I'm sorry. Here."

"Thank you." The blonde woman dabbed at her nose before raising her steely blue gaze to Hud. "Detective, is it possible for me to see him? When will he be released to the funeral home?"

Hud pulled out his cell phone. "I'll call the ME's office and find out where they are in the process."

"Thank you." While he stepped into the foyer to make his call, Doris opened the liquor cabinet, inspected the display of bottles and then selected one. She held up the bottle of Irish whiskey for Gigi to see and then set out three glasses. "This was his favorite. Would you join me in a toast?"

"No, thank you."

"Detective?"

"I'm on duty, ma'am." Hud smiled an apology and returned to his call.

"Then I'll do this on my own." Doris poured herself a shot and raised her glass to the portrait over the mantel. "To Ian. You weren't a great husband. But for thirty years, you were mine." She downed the amber liquid in one smooth swallow before closing her eyes and hugging the empty glass to her chest. Gigi's head was bowed in respect to the private moment when the glass clinked against the tray in the liquor cabinet, startling her. The moment of reverence ended as Doris crossed the room. "Now. What is it you wanted me to show you?"

Though not exactly the way Gigi expected a widow to grieve, she knew every individual had his or her own process to deal with the loss. She unfolded a slip of paper where she'd written down the numbers Ian had given her and handed it to Doris. "Do these numbers mean anything to you?"

Doris pulled her glasses from her purse and read over them. "The first six match the combination to Ian's safe. But there are too many other numbers here. I don't know what they are. Unless…" Infused with a sudden energy, she went to a smaller painting hanging on the wall and pulled it open like a door to reveal a safe. She turned the combination dial and lifted the handle to open it. "Maybe that old goat was thinking about me at the end, after all." She sorted through a stack of plastic folders inside, pulling out different ones to compare numbers. With each comparison, her shoulders sagged a little more. Eventually, she replaced the entire stack and turned a sad smile to Gigi. "It's not the insurance policies or investment portfolios." She studied the paper one more time before handing it back to Gigi. "I'm stumped. How did you get these numbers?"

Gigi slipped the paper into her pocket. "Ian gave them to me. But he never said what they were. Do you know why he would do that?"

"Maybe he thought I wouldn't remember the combination. The rest I can't explain." Doris glanced at the contents of the safe again. "Do you want to look?"

The older woman stepped back as Gigi peeked into the cube-shaped recess in the wall. Besides the legal documents Doris had mentioned, there were embossed leather jewelry cases and a semiautomatic handgun with a lock wedged into the trigger. Although the weapon gave her some pause, Gigi's pulse rate kicked up a notch at the ten flash drives stored in a clear plastic box. "What are those?"

Doris pulled out the rectangular box. "Papers Ian wrote. His notes on various projects. I confess, even if I could open the files, I wouldn't understand the science. He shared my love for the theater—we used to have season tickets to the Kauffman Center. But I never quite understood his obsession with math and tinkering. Here." She handed Gigi the box. "Maybe they'll mean something to you. Or they'll be useful to the lab."

"Are you sure?" She cradled the plastic between her hands, already calculating what the documentation inside could mean. "I don't have a warrant to take them."

Doris patted Gigi's hand and smiled. "It's a gift. He'd want you to have them. He often spoke of you as though you were his scientific muse. Perhaps even a daughter. We never had children, you know."

"Thank you, Doris. He meant a lot to me, too." She leaned in to hug the older woman, as grateful for the gift as she was anxious to find out if it could help her solve the riddle of Ian's formula. "I'm honored to have them."

"If there's a Nobel Prize in there, you let me know." Gigi couldn't tell if that was a soft laugh or another sniffle as Doris pulled away. Her gaze was trained beyond Gigi's shoulder. "Your detective friend is waiting for you. You'd better go. I have phone calls to make."

"Will you be all right here by yourself?"

"I won't be alone for long. My attorney will be stopping by soon. Thank you." Doris pulled Gigi in for another quick hug before leading her to the front door. "For everything."

When they met up in the foyer, Hud relayed the information Doris needed from the ME's office and escorted Gigi out to the truck. She was so excited to dive into this new possibility that Hud had to quicken his pace to keep up with her long strides. "What's that?"

"Answers, I hope." As soon as she was seated inside, Gigi opened the box and studied the labels on each flash drive. She didn't need the paper to compare it to, but she pulled it out to make her point to Hud the moment he closed the driver's-side door behind him. "If the first numbers are the combination to the safe, then the next one could be…" She pulled out the one that matched. "Hopefully, the rest of those numbers can get me into whatever files are on this."

"Look at you goin' all Nancy Drew on me." He started the engine while she buckled in. "Interesting catch about the coat, too. While I was on the phone with Niall, I snuck a peek inside the hall closet."

"And?"

"There were three women's coats hanging there. She must own stock in the coat market if she has another she can afford to leave on a plane." He drove around the circular driveway and pulled into the street.

"Is that important?"

"What does your gut tell you? You noticed it for a reason."

Not that she trusted her gut, but the incongruence did bother her. "We need to call the airline to find out if her coat is in the lost and found. Or if she was even on that plane."

Hud tapped the side of his nose in a universal sign that she'd gotten it right.

"But why? Surely, you don't suspect her. Doris seemed genuinely upset."

"So did Hana Nowak. So did you." He looked at her across the cab of the truck. "There's only one of you I trust has told me the truth about everything."

"Me, right?"

His laughter filled up the truck and Gigi smiled.

But the respite was brief. Before Hud could dial Keir's number, her own phone rang. The urge to laugh vanished and fear chilled her blood. "What if it's him?"

Hud turned off onto a side street and parked against the curb. "Put it on speaker."

She pulled her phone from her backpack and answered. "This is Professor Brennan."

Hud reached across the console to squeeze Gigi's hand as she recoiled from the low, ominous breathing that answered. With his free hand, he texted Keir to trace the incoming call.

"Did you find what I needed?" the weird, distorted voice asked.

"Not yet." Hud silently signaled for her to keep the conversation going. "I'm working on it. I might have a new lead. But it will take time to decipher—"

"Time is a luxury you don't have, Virginia." With each beat of silence that passed, the tension inside Gigi knotted tighter and tighter. "I know Lombard's widow gave you something. Is it my formula?"

"How did you know…?"

Hudson swore. The artificial voice laughed. "I hear your boyfriend is with you."

Hud unholstered his gun and texted the word *BOLO* to Keir Watson—be on the lookout for. The creep must have followed them, could be following them right now. He said he'd be watching. Hud pushed open his door and checked up and down the street.

The laughter ended abruptly. "He can look, but he won't find me. He won't be able to protect you or the people you love. As a matter of fact, I have eyes on your sister right now. Looks like she had a fun trip to Vegas."

Gigi's terror erupted in a burst of anger. "You stay away from her! I'm working as hard as I can. You'll have Ian's formula. Monday morning at six, just like you said."

Hud climbed back in as soon as he heard the threat and dialed his partner. He wasn't wasting time on a text.

"Don't disappoint me," the voice warned.

"I won't. I promise. Just leave Tammy alone."

But the line had already gone silent.

"Hud?" Her hands were shaking too badly to keep hold of her phone. "He's going to hurt her."

Hud shifted his truck into Drive and spoke the moment Keir picked up. "Gigi just got another call from the perp."

"We're tracking it."

"Where is Tammy Brennan?"

"The officer I assigned to her is with her at Gigi's

house right now. She's picking up clothes and toiletries."

"Secure her in the house," Hud ordered. "Perp said he had eyes on her."

"I'll alert Officer Logan and send backup."

"How can he know we were just at Doris Lombard's *and* have eyes on my house?"

"Two perps, remember? Hell. Between the two of them, they've probably seen every move we've made." Hud reached beneath his seat and pulled out a magnetic portable siren. He stuck it on top of the truck and turned on the lights and the shrill alarm, picking up speed with every passing block as they raced across the city. "Hold on."

She nodded.

"Get out of your head, G," he warned. "Don't you be thinkin' the worst."

"How can I not? I have to work a scientific miracle or else he'll hurt her."

"Reach inside my jacket pocket," he instructed, nodding toward the leather jacket she still wore. "My pen and notebook are in there. Keep your hands busy. Keep your mind focused."

She thrust her hands inside the deep pockets and curled her fingers around the items there. It was a ridiculous exercise, under the circumstances, but it worked. Hud's scent, something to focus on, the fact that he'd listened and observed and remembered what helped her cope with the panic worked.

"You with me?" he asked, never taking his eyes off the road.

"I'm okay," she answered. And she meant it.

They were sailing through a red light on Brush Creek Parkway when Keir called back. "I'm en route to Gigi's house now. Logan has it locked down tight. You were right. Gigi's caller used a burner phone. Looks like it was turned off immediately after the call so we couldn't pinpoint an exact location. But I can narrow it down and tell you what cell tower it pinged off."

"And?" Hud cursed when he didn't get an instant response. "Where did it come from?"

"Gigi's neighborhood."

## Chapter Eleven

Gigi raced up the steps to her front porch. She barely had the key inserted into the lock when the door swung open. "Tam…"

She retreated a step as a twentysomething black man in a KCPD uniform filled the doorway. "Are you Gigi Brennan, ma'am?"

"Yes." Her feet danced with panic after hearing those threats. But his raised hand stopped her from sliding past him to get inside. "Who are you? Where's my sister?"

"Officer Albert Logan." She felt Hud at her back as the tall, muscular officer included them both in his warning. "I'm sorry. I need to see your identification."

"This is my house. Tammy?" She patted her pockets. Of course, her billfold wasn't there. "My backpack is in the truck."

"Easy, G." Hud caught her before she could dash to the truck where they'd parked at the curb and turned her to the front door. He flashed his badge to the young officer. "Detective Kramer. I've got lead on this case. Keir Watson is my partner. Glad to see you're doing your job, but I need her inside and out of sight ASAP."

"Is that Gigi, Al?" She heard a familiar voice shouting from upstairs.

Albert Logan's stern expression relaxed into a smile. "He said you were the only cop I could let in besides him." He stepped back and held the door open. "Sorry for the delay, ma'am. She's upstairs."

Gigi bolted up the stairs to her sister's bedroom suite. "Tammy?"

"Right here, you big worrywart." Tammy met her in her doorway, her strawberry-blond hair pulled back into a ponytail, her beautiful smile fixed firmly in place.

Gigi swallowed her up in a tight hug. "Are you all right? What are you doing here? You're supposed to be in protective custody."

"I need clothes." Tammy squeezed her right back. "Al picked me up at the airport and is going to drive me to a safe house." As she pulled away, Tammy's blue gaze shifted to Hud who'd followed her up the stairs. Since Gigi had gotten all the shy genes in the family, Tammy extended her hand and offered him a smile. "So, who's this bad boy you brought with you? I'm Tammy Brennan. We've met before, haven't we?"

Hud smiled back. "Hudson Kramer, KCPD. You have a good memory. The Shamrock Bar, a couple years back. You bought my partner and me a drink. Your sister tagged along and kicked my ass playin' pool."

Tammy's mouth rounded with a big O before she pointed to him and whispered, "He's the guy?"

"The guy?" Hud echoed.

Gigi shushed her sister's excitement. She'd mentioned her crush on Hud a time or two over the years, but she didn't realize how much Tammy had actually listened.

Tammy propped her hands at the waist of her snug jeans and beamed a smile at Hud. "This *is* an interesting development. That explains the gym bag with a change of men's clothes in the downstairs bathroom."

Gigi reached back to take Hud's hand. "Sorry about that. She doesn't have a filter."

"Nosy much?" Hud teased, linking his fingers with hers and not looking one bit self-conscious about the innuendos Tammy had thrown his way.

Tammy hugged Gigi to her side. "Hey, she's not the only Brennan with a curious mind. I'm just the extroverted version."

"I can see that." And just like that, Hud shifted from teasing charmer into cop mode. "You haven't noticed anyone following you? Received any threats?"

Tammy released Gigi and crossed to the open suitcase lying on the bed. "Your partner asked me the same questions. No and no. Then he said Gigi was in danger and introduced me to Al. Said he was going to be my shadow for a while. Between your messages and calls from Detective Watson, I'm happy to have the company." She paused in the middle of rolling up a pair of slacks. "You're keeping my big sister safe?"

"I'm doing my best." Hud's hand squeezed around Gigi's, silently making sure she was all right before excusing himself from the conversation. "I'll leave you two to finish packing. I'll be downstairs getting a sitrep from Officer Logan."

"Tell Al I'll only be a few more minutes." Tammy tossed her pants into the suitcase and followed him out the door to watch him go down the stairs. "Nice butt."

"Tammy!"

"Oh, relax. I'm happy for you." Tammy strolled back into the room to resume her packing. "It's about time my big sister found a guy to shack up with."

Gigi's thoughts short-circuited. "We are not shacking... We're working together on a police investigation. Brains and brawn."

"He's definitely got the brawny part down." She stuffed socks into her running shoes and added them to her suitcase. "I wonder if he'd make a good big brother."

"He would. He has three younger siblings. His parents died and he raised them just like I... Oh. You." The recitation of Hud's history ended when she saw the cheese-eating grin on her sister's face. "Give me a break, okay. This relationship stuff isn't anything I've ever studied in a classroom."

Tammy waved off the reprimanding tone and closed her suitcase. "You don't learn this kind of stuff from a book. You learn it by living it. Although, this murder/blackmail scenario isn't exactly the meet-cute I'd go for."

"Meet-cute?"

"My point is, if you like Hud and he likes you, then go for it. After all you've given up in your life—for your studies, for me—nobody deserves a happily-ever-after more."

"I don't know if this is long-term. This situation has thrown us together and intensified things. I like him. And I think he kind of likes me."

Tammy carried her suitcase to the doorway and glanced down the stairs. "Oh, sweetie, he likes you a lot. He barely took his eyes off you until he left the room. And even then, he didn't want to go."

Was that true? Did Hud watch her the way she sometimes watched him? She touched the temple of her glasses. "He's protective of me."

"Another reason I like him." Tammy took her hand and sat on the bench at the foot of her bed, pulling Gigi down beside her. "I know I'm not the best person to give relationship advice, but I do know you. I've never known anyone who was more of a one-man kind of woman than you are. I know how hard trust is for you, how hard it is for you to come out of your shell and embrace your emotions. You've already let Detective Kramer in. I saw you reach for him instead of sticking your hands into your pockets and dealing with all this chaos on your own. He's your one."

Her sister's earnest blue eyes saw things more clearly than Gigi had. A one-man kind of woman. That made sense with her aversion to Gary. He wasn't the one. Hudson Kramer was that man. He always had been. All the logic in the world couldn't explain it, but she was in love with Hud.

"Look at the annoying little sister being the smart one for a change." Gigi was a little uncomfortable with both this role reversal and the acceptance of her feelings for Hud. "What do I do about it?"

"What do you want to do?"

"I want to be with him. In every way."

Tammy slid her arm around Gigi's waist and led her into the bathroom. "Okay, then. I have two bits of advice. One, I know you're not on the pill. Even though I am, I keep a box of condoms in here beside the sink." She opened the drawer and set the box in Gigi's hand. "You're the one who taught me to be safe. Help yourself."

"I don't need that kind of advice. I know how things work." She stuffed the box back into its drawer and closed it. "What's number two?"

"In my experience, men can be pretty thickheaded. You have to tell them plain and simple exactly what you want and how you feel. Can you have that kind of conversation with him?"

"I think so."

"Wow. He really is the one." Tammy stretched up to give Gigi a big hug. "You'll be a rock star with this guy—I can tell."

Hud called from the bottom of the stairs. "Time to go, ladies. Officer Logan is waiting out front."

Reluctantly, Gigi pulled away. "I wish I could be the big sister who gives you this kind of advice, instead of the other way around."

"No worries. We both have our skill sets. If you weren't as practical and driven as you are, I wouldn't have a college degree or a career. I might not even have a roof over my head. You don't have to gossip or be girly-girl with me. You were there for me, Gigi. You provided for me. You gave me a safe, solid foundation so I could go out and be the wild-and-crazy girl that I am. You took care of me and made us a family. That's how I know you love me."

"I do." They traded another quick hug. "The idea of this man hurting you... I want you to be safe, okay?"

"Don't worry about me. I think Al looks pretty capable if anybody gets too close." She shrugged into her jacket, picked up her purse and suitcase, and headed downstairs. "I love you, too. Now, wrap up this whole murder-crime thingy, get your man and call me when you have time to bake some cookies and stay up late and talk. I'm dying to tell you about my adventure in Vegas."

Gigi followed Tammy to the porch where Hud was waiting for them. Officer Logan picked up Tammy's suitcase and carried it to his squad car at the end of the driveway, where he popped the trunk to stow it inside. "Am I going to like this story?"

"Probably not. But I won four hundred dollars and the guy was cute."

"You're hopeless."

Tammy trotted down the steps, walking past her yellow Volkswagen on her way to the squad car. "I'd like to think I'm hopeful—"

*Boom.*

One second, she was smiling, the next, Tammy was flying through the air as her car exploded. A wave of heat collided with Gigi. She hit the painted white planks of the porch hard, knocking the breath from her lungs. Hud landed beside her, then rolled on top of her, shielding her with his body as fire, metal and glass rained down around them. Whatever he shouted in her ear, she couldn't hear.

She could only hold on and pray her sister wasn't dead.

GIGI PACED THE CORRIDOR outside Tammy's room at Saint Luke's Hospital. The hour was late, and Tammy needed her rest, but Gigi wanted to hear one more report from the doctor checking on her and tell Tammy she loved her again before saying good-night.

Keir Watson and his wife, Kenna, had stopped by the house to get Gigi a pair of jeans, a blouse and a sweater to change into. They'd brought Hud clean clothes as well, along with a preliminary report from the crime-scene technicians and the grim news that Tammy's car had been remotely detonated by a cell phone wired into the explosives.

A neat trick any engineer or physicist could put together.

She knew at least two men with a beef against Ian Lombard who could pull that off. There were also Lukin dissidents and terrorists and drug smugglers all over the world who'd be willing to plant a bomb in exchange for Ian's formula and the potential weapons and industrial machinery that could be made from it.

The blast could have been the result of random timing. But she believed, and Hud agreed, that whoever had dialed that number had been watching the house, timing it perfectly to injure Tammy and terrorize Gigi. A few seconds sooner, and Tammy might have been killed. A few seconds later, Tammy would have been gone and Gigi wouldn't have witnessed the explosion and the damage done to her own sense of security.

Gigi reached the end of the corridor, turned and paced back past Hud and Keir and Kenna, each of them on their phones, working some angle on the investigation with the crime lab, the KCPD patrol division and the district attorney's office. She walked toward Tammy's room and the grim expression of the uniformed guard standing watch outside her door. Albert Logan's squad car had protected him from the blast. But it couldn't protect him from the guilt he must be feeling—the same guilt Gigi felt. That bomb could have been placed there at any time over the past twenty-four hours. Maybe that was even part of what the two intruders had been up to the night before. As Gigi walked by, she reached out and squeezed Albert's forearm. His dark hand covered hers for a moment.

"Not your fault," she whispered, and kept walking.

"Yours either, ma'am." She nodded her thanks but wondered if Albert believed it any more than she did.

The momentary deafness caused by the concussive blast had faded away, but there still seemed to be a shroud covering her brain, preventing clear thought from coming through. None of her own scrapes and cuts were serious, but she still felt off-kilter.

Tammy had been the closest to the exploding car, but she'd been far enough away that none of her injuries were life-threatening. Still, with a broken arm, a bruised kidney and multiple lacerations, the doctors wanted to keep her in the hospital overnight for observation and rest. Life-threatening or not, Tammy's injuries filled Gigi with fear and ignited an anger that needed a place to channel before she started screaming or broke down into tears.

That's why when her phone rang and she recognized the number, she answered before Hud could stop her. "What do you want?" she demanded, hitting the speaker button as Hud abruptly ended his call and ushered her into the empty room across the hall. "I'm doing what you asked. You didn't have to hurt my sister."

"That could have been you."

"You're not motivating me. You're pissing me off." Gigi heard herself shouting but couldn't seem to rein in her emotions.

The hollow voice laughed. "The great Virginia Brennan does have a trigger, after all. Can I tell you how satisfying it is to hear you lose it?"

"Who is this? Gary? Evgeni? I won't give you what you want."

Hud's golden eyes locked onto hers, warning her she was pushing the caller too far. Or maybe wondering if she really was losing it.

The caller refused to answer her accusations. Instead, he filled the small hospital room with the insidious sound of that mechanically distorted breathing. Then he calmly reminded her that he was the one controlling her life. "Let me tell you how angry I'll be if you don't give me what I want. I can get to your sister in the hospital. A simple injection, and she could have an embolism in her lung or heart. She could suffocate under a pillow or receive the wrong medication."

"You son of a bitch."

"Language, Virginia. No more noble defiance. You bring me what I want, or Tammy dies."

"I'll be there. But if you threaten my family again…"

The click of his disconnect felt like a slap in the face. The anger and frustration grew too strong for her to control and she cocked her arm back, ready to sling her phone across the room.

But a saner figure caught her wrist, plucked her phone from her grip and pulled her tight against his chest. "I've got you, G. You have the right to be angry. You're exhausted. It's okay to be afraid." She pounded her fist against Hud's shoulder until the tears came. And when the emotional outburst had run its course, his cool lips grazed her forehead. "You with me?"

She nodded. Then she cupped his stubbled jaw and looked into those green-gold eyes to read the steady reassurance there. "I freaked out on you again, didn't I."

His smile didn't quite reach his eyes. "I bet you do that to all the guys."

She laughed as he meant her to, but wasn't quite feeling the humor, either. She brushed her lips against his and hugged him again. "You're an anchor for me. I don't think I could get through these forty-eight hours without you."

"Yep, I always wanted to be the heavy chunk of iron hanging around some woman's neck."

She went stiff in his arms. "I'm sorry. That doesn't sound like a compliment. But to me, it was."

"It's okay, G." His words took on a bittersweet tone as he pulled away. But he wrapped his hand around hers and they walked into the hallway together. "The doctor should be done by now. Let's say good-night to Tammy and get you home for a decent night's sleep. That hour we got this morning won't cut it. You're workin' a miracle tomorrow, remember?"

"No pressure, huh?"

After the doctor's reassurance that rest and follow-up visits with the specialists who'd worked on her were the only medicine Tammy needed, the sisters traded hugs and said good-night.

Despite the cuts and bruises on her face, Tammy smiled as she lay back on her pillow. "You go get these guys, sis. And, Hud? Take care of her."

"I will," Hud promised, giving her free hand a squeeze. "Rest up, kiddo. We'll check in on you tomorrow before you're taken to the safe house."

While Gigi dimmed the lights and closed the door, Hud took Albert Logan aside and pointed his finger in the young officer's face. "You do not leave your post unless this man—" he pointed to Keir "—or someone he introduces to you personally relieves you. No one goes into that room except for medical professionals, and then you go in with them. Tammy is not to be left alone. Understood?"

"She won't be."

"Good man." After a friendly smack on the shoulder, he turned to Keir. "You got this?"

Keir nodded. "We'll keep her safe, Gigi, I promise."

"Thank you, Keir." Hud wasn't the only man she was learning to trust. Gigi held out her hand and felt herself being pulled in for a brotherly hug.

"You keep an eye on this tough guy, okay? I'll handle the rest."

"I'll do my best."

When the hug ended, Hud slipped her backpack onto her shoulder and took her hand to lead her to the elevators and down to the parking garage.

Once they were inside his truck and the heater was running, Hud turned to her. The yellowish lights of the garage cast an unnatural glow across the rugged angles of his face. But his golden eyes were tender, familiar. "What do you need tonight? Food? Rest?"

Gigi leaned back against the headrest, wishing that climbing over the center console and cuddling in Hud's lap was an option. She exhaled a deep breath and felt weariness consume her. "I need to think. I'll figure out the damn formula. But not if I can't… think…because my brain is overloaded with this helplessness and anger."

He reached across the cab to tuck a strand of hair behind her ear. "You are anything but helpless. Everything's in motion from our end. We'll have officers undercover in the Front Street area early Monday morning, and a SWAT team on standby. And I will be right there with you."

She turned her cheek into his lingering hand. "I don't want anyone else to get hurt."

"Not gonna happen, G. The trap will be set. We'll get this guy and his accomplice." He reversed out of the parking space and followed the arrows up to the street-level exit. They merged with the lights and traffic of Saturday night on the Plaza before he suddenly grinned and filled the cab of the truck with his infectious energy. "You said you need time and space to think."

"Uh-huh."

"Home or office?"

What was going on in that handsome head of his? "Where would you feel more comfortable?"

It was hard not to smile when he seemed so delighted with whatever he was planning. "Home, I guess, considering everyone I work with is a suspect."

"Burgers or pizza?"

Her stomach rumbled at the mention of food, reminding her they hadn't eaten since they'd shared coffee and doughnuts that morning. "Pizza."

"Sleep or sex?"

The choice shocked her. Excited her. "Could I have both?"

They pulled up to a stoplight and Hud leaned across the console to press a quick, hard kiss to her lips. "Now you're thinkin'."

She leaned back in her seat as the light turned green. "Wait. You were just trying to distract me, weren't you? Get me out of my head?"

He chuckled. "You feel better, don't you?"

Deflated to learn this was some kind of game, yet strangely energized by the fun banter and possibilities, Gigi swatted his arm. "You stink, Hudson Kramer."

He caught her hand before she could pull away and brought it to his lips to kiss her knuckles. The scrape of his beard tickled her skin, but his promise seeped in and warmed her from head to toe. "It'll happen, G. I wouldn't offer if I wasn't serious. I want it, too."

She was a quick study. She could play the game, too. "So, you're saying you want sleep?"

"Dr. Brennan—if you weren't such a complete brainiac detached from your emotions and too shy to spit out a complete coherent sentence when you get nervous, I'd think you were flirtin' with me."

She weighed the accurate, yet faintly disparaging words against his sly tone. "Teasing?"

He winked.

She'd never flirted with a man before, had she? It was fun to see the pink coloring his cheeks. "Well, I do have three college degrees, so you know I like learning new things. My research tells me that you'd be an excellent teacher."

His answering groan might well be the sexiest sound she'd ever heard him make. "You sure it's me you want?"

She didn't have to think about it, and she was no longer afraid to admit it. "I've never thought about it being anyone else but you."

The traffic thinned out and he pumped on the accelerator. "Pizza first."

"Because I'm going to need my strength?"

He laughed out loud. "No. I think I am."

GIGI PUT AWAY three slices of a hamburger-and-mushroom pizza and two molasses cookies before she picked up the remote and paused the movie she and Hud were watching. With her long legs stretched to the coffee table in front of them, and an afghan covering her from shoulder to stockinged toe, Hud had hoped she'd fall asleep. Then he could safely put her to bed and grab that cold shower he'd been thinking about ever since she'd called his bluff and said yes to having sex with him. He didn't think he'd ever wanted a thing as badly as he wanted to feel Gigi fly apart in his arms as they explored the chemistry that no text-book could fully teach her.

But tonight wasn't about him. None of this week-end was about him and what he wanted. His official job was to unmask a pair of killers and keep KCPD's greatest asset for getting the job done safe. His unof-ficial job was to listen and comfort or prod or protect or be whatever Gigi needed so she could complete Lombard's formula and bait the trap to arrest them.

"Tammy said I needed to tell you exactly what I want."

Not the opening to a conversation that he'd ex-pected. But he was learning that Gigi's complex brain sometimes took the scenic route to get to the point she wanted to make. He picked up another cookie from the plate on the coffee table and leaned back against the opposite corner of the sofa to munch on the dec-adent treat. "You're taking relationship advice from Tammy? The woman who picks up guys in bars and comes home with secrets from a teachers' conference in Las Vegas?"

"Yes." She curled her legs beneath her and turned to face him. "Growing up, I wasn't the normal one, Hud. Tammy could always make friends and interact with people. She's learned a lot more about relation-ships and human nature than I ever have. She's like you. She has instincts about people, and embraces her feelings about them." She tapped the side of her head. "I have to logically figure everything out."

Hud swallowed his cookie and turned off the TV. Apparently, sleep and a cold shower weren't going to happen. "Then talk to me. Let's figure this out together. What did Tammy want you to tell me?"

"Someone just tried to kill her. You and I might not live past Monday morning. My whole life has been put on hold while I earn degrees and bury my parents and raise my sister. Even if I'd had a normal life, I've been too introverted and too intellectual to get out of my head and be brave about going after what I want."

Hud mirrored her position on the couch. With his gun and badge on the coffee table beside the cookies, he gave himself permission to answer as a man, not a cop. "There's nobody braver than you, G. You lead a research team and teach a lecture hall full of students, even though it's a challenge for you. A coward would have folded at the first sign of trouble with your boss's murder. You came to me—at the crime scene, at the police station—to help find his killer. You kissed me when I was too stubborn, too afraid to risk feeling something for a woman again. Don't you ever tell me you're not brave."

He waited for her to touch her glasses to settle whatever nerves she was feeling. But her hands remained clasped on top of the afghan in her lap. "Then…if I said I wanted you to make love to me tonight…you'd be okay with that?"

"Don't want to die a virgin, hmm?" He waved aside that comment, regretting the words the moment they left his mouth. "Sorry. Bad joke. Those are my defenses talking." If she could be brave enough to share what she was feeling, then he owed it to her to do the same. He slid across the couch until he could touch the soft skin of her cheek and run his fingers through the auburn silk of her hair. He found the clip at the back of her head and unhooked it, letting that long waterfall of hair tumble through his fingers. "I'd be very okay with that."

He knew he had a history of being quick to give his heart to a woman who needed him. But this felt different. Never in a million years would he have thought a woman like Gigi and he could work. But tonight, he felt like all the missteps with other women, all the lousy timing and bad luck, all those trips to the friend zone had simply prepared him for this one woman. He desperately needed to get everything right this time. The thought of another man touching her the way she'd just asked him to made him a little crazy. He wanted every first touch, every first anything with her. He'd become the Gigi-whisperer, yeah. But she'd done something for him, too. Gigi had gotten under his skin, gotten into his head, gotten into his heart. Meeting her was the best kind of luck a man could have.

Gigi made him feel like he was enough.

He tugged on the back of her neck. "Come here."

When he fell back onto the couch and she landed on top of him and kissed him, he knew he was more than enough. Her legs tangled with his and her long hair fell around his face and shoulders. Her fingers curled into his shirt, digging into the skin underneath. His hands found a palmful of her bottom and the back of her head to align her body and mouth with his. Her small breasts beaded against his chest as her lips parted over his, and their tongues danced together.

His body was primed, and the woman was willing. She tasted of cookies and smelled like his favorite pizza. He released her only long enough to pull the bulky afghan from in between them, and then he was back, tugging her blouse loose and then sliding his hands against cool skin, stroking up along her back before dipping beneath the waist of her jeans and panties. Still, he needed more.

He sat up, spilling Gigi into his lap, freeing his hands to push the sweater she wore off her shoulders. The blouse came next. If she wanted to wrap herself in something, it was going to be him.

Hud sampled his way over the point of her chin, down the long column of her neck. He pressed a kiss to the soft swell of skin above her white satin bra and then dipped his head to take the nipple into his mouth, wetting her through the material, loving how she squirmed in his lap and then raked her fingers into his hair to hold his mouth against the straining tip while she whispered his name.

Then Gigi pulled his mouth back to hers, demanding a kiss while her fingers fumbled with his belt buckle. "Hud…" she whispered against his mouth, tugging on his shirt. "I can't get…" She slipped her hands beneath his shirt, the needy caress of skin upon skin making him shudder. "I want…"

"Me, too."

Moments later, they were naked in her bed. Hud

rolled on a condom and pushed inside her, holding himself still as she adjusted to the feel of him filling her. He'd made her writhe with his hands and his mouth. But she'd insisted it wasn't enough, that she needed him, needed all of him. Her little cry of pain when he entered her nearly stopped him. But she buried her face against his shoulder and breathed such a warm, satisfied sigh against his skin that he swelled inside her.

Then she lay back against the pillow, her mussed-up hair falling in a halo around her head. With her glasses on the bedside table, it was easy to see the desire darkening her eyes. "I want more."

She was definitely a fast learner. That siren call was irresistible.

"Like this?" Bracing himself on his elbows above her, he pulled gently out of her, then pressed inside again, her slick walls taking him in, easing the friction as he moved faster and faster, and grew harder and harder with every thrust.

"I know the basics." Her voice was a breathless gasp against his ear. There was nothing basic about the way she made him feel. She hugged him around the neck, skimmed her hands over his shoulders and back, nipped at his chin and jaw and earlobe until his heart pounded in his chest and every nerve ending primed him for release. "But isn't there something I can do for you? How can I make it better?"

"You can't, G. This is about as mind-blowing as it gets." Her hips squirmed beneath him and he knew she was about to come. He squeezed his eyes shut, determined to make this last, determined to make this good for her.

She grabbed his face, turning his gaze down to hers. "What do you want me to do?"

"It's a fantasy of mine. I shouldn't. Not your first time."

"What? Tell me." She lifted her head and kissed him squarely on the mouth. "Tell me."

"Wrap your legs around me. Stretch yourself open. Hold me with your…body." He gulped in the middle of that sentence because she did exactly that. He slipped in a fraction deeper and nearly lost it then as her body gripped his.

"Like this?"

"Yeah… Just like…" Her heels linked behind him, pulling herself into his helpless thrust. "Gorgeous… legs…"

"Can't you talk…either? That feels…" She raised her hips to meet the next plunge.

He quickened the pace. Her body shook. Her fingers dug into his skin as her back arched. "Let it happen, honey. Let it happen."

He buried his face against her neck and she shuddered all around him, crying out his name.

He followed after, losing himself in the pleasure and warmth and welcome that was G.

After fetching a washcloth to clean them both, and retrieving his gun to set it within arm's reach on the bedside table, Hud climbed beneath the covers and spooned his naked body behind hers. He smoothed her hair away from the dampness at the nape of her neck and kissed her there. "You okay?"

She seemed boneless and completely spent. "I've never been this okay in my life."

He chuckled, then had to put a firm hand on her hip to stop her from rubbing her bottom against him. Whether she was simply trying to find a comfortable position to sleep, or he'd awakened the irresistible tigress in her, they both needed time to rest before they tried this combustible chemistry experiment again. "Easy, G. You may be a little sore for a while. I'm guessing you've used some muscles you never have before."

Her fingers moved tentatively along his forearm around her waist. "What about you? Was I all right? Did you enjoy it, too?"

"I don't think *all right* is big enough for what I'm feeling. What are some big words you know? Marvelous? Stupendous? Horny as hell and ready for more?"

"I'm serious, Hud." She gave him a playful elbow to the gut for teasing her as his list continued.

"Sated? Superlative? Splendiferous?"

"Perfect."

## Chapter Twelve

Hud tried hard not to feel cast aside when he woke up to find the bed empty and cool beside him.

Maybe last night had just been about a woman wanting to get her virginity card off the table, and he'd been the guy she trusted enough to give herself to. Or maybe last night had been the ultimate Gigi-whisperer exercise. If a touch could distract her from her thoughts, a kiss could center her, then making love with all that incredible, full-body contact must have cleared her brain to come up with the next Nobel Prize for Physics.

Could he have been wrong about her? Maybe she *was* the kind of woman to take what she needed from him, then back off from any relationship blossoming between them. And maybe this had nothing to do with him at all. When he pulled on his jeans and followed the smell of coffee and bacon to the kitchen where she was sitting cross-legged in a chair at the table, poring over her laptop, he reminded himself that she was a unique human being, far more comfortable with those brainy calculations he didn't understand than with her emotions. And with a deadline barreling down on her in fewer than twenty-four hours, he couldn't blame her for wanting to get an early start.

"Morning." Still, when her only response to his greeting was a nod and a point toward the scones sitting on a platter on top of the stove, it was difficult to believe that last night had meant the same thing to Gigi that it did to him.

He spotted the box of flash drives on the table beside her and told himself that the woman had her priorities straight. Instead of assessing his wounded ego, he popped a slice of crispy bacon into his mouth and carried the teakettle over to top off Gigi's mug.

She barely looked away from the screen to drop the tea bag and strainer back into her mug. "Thanks."

Communication. That was a good sign, right?

"Did you find anything?" he asked.

She picked up the nearly used-up legal pad she'd been writing on and flipped to a new page to jot down a series of numbers and symbols. "I got the flash drive to open."

At least one mystery had been solved. "The string of numbers was the combination to his safe, the label on the flash drive—"

"And the encryption code." Just like two nights ago at the precinct, she was obsessed with writing and drawing and scratching out and writing again.

He'd better leave her to her work. After all, she was the brains of this operation. He couldn't help her with any of that. He carried the kettle back to the stove, poured himself a mug of coffee and devoured a buttery lemon scone that pricked his taste buds and melted down his throat. Wow. In so many ways, Gigi really was the woman of his dreams.

But right now, she didn't need him. Reminding himself that there was work he could be doing, too, he grabbed another scone and headed to the bathroom to run hot water for a shower and a shave.

Fifteen minutes later, he stepped out of the shower, wrapped a towel around his waist and realized he wasn't alone. Gigi stood inside the bathroom door, curling her toes in the throw rug there. For a split second, excitement surged through his veins. Had she come to join him?

But then he saw her arms locked around her waist in a tight hug, and a different kind of heat put him on full alert. Something was majorly wrong. Had she gotten another phone call from that terrorizing thug? From the hospital? Was there someone breaking in? Just how long would it take him to get his gun from the bedroom next door?

Then she touched her glasses and her eyes zeroed in on his. "It won't work."

Hud was already crossing the room. He squeezed his hands around her shoulders, reassuring himself that she wasn't hurt or in any immediate danger.

She was upset about something, though. He could feel her trembling. If he wasn't still soaking wet, he'd pull her into his arms. "What are you talking about?"

"Ian's formula. It won't work."

Hud retreated a step. Not the bad news he'd expected. "How do you know?"

"Because I'm really smart."

That was a given. "I mean, what's wrong with it?"

"His equations don't balance. I found a mistake. His heat ratio is off." Her gaze swept across his chest and down to the edge of the towel below his belly button before she averted her head to face the toilet. "I have to go to the lab."

"Not a problem. I'll be ready in ten minutes and can take you there."

When he reached around her to open the door, she stopped him with a palm against his chest. He felt that touch like a brand and wondered if her fingers had been singed by the same heat he felt. "And I'll need you to put on a shirt because I can't think when you're naked like this."

At last. This was the woman hidden inside Professor Brennan that he'd needed to see this morning. No longer caring if he dripped on her, Hud leaned in to seal his lips to hers in a gentle kiss. "Imagine how I felt last night when I got to see and touch all of you."

Her fingers tested the smooth skin of his jaw after his shave in the shower. "I don't know how to deal with the morning after—what I'm supposed to say or do. Tammy didn't tell me and I didn't think to ask. But it was wonderful and thank you and I'd do it again and—"

"It's okay, G." He pressed a finger to her lips and smiled. "We'll figure us out later. Right now, I need to get you to the lab."

Hud watched Gigi do her thing in the lab. With spare parts cannibalized from other devices, a mix of compounds from a storage cabinet, wires and microchips and commands typed into her laptop, Gigi had accomplished in three hours what a top-of-the-line mechanic could do to his truck in an entire week.

Even though Hud stood at the entryway to the lab, several feet from the table where Gigi was building her high-tech contraption, to keep an eye out for any unexpected visitors, she'd insisted he put on a pair of safety goggles. Now he was glad he had.

"Firing up the mobile power bank," she announced, pushing a button on her computer. At first nothing happened. Then the capacitor started to hum. She disconnected her computer and set it on a nearby table, allowing Lombard's design to generate its own power. He followed the connecting cords to the hot plate with a large glass beaker filled with water sitting on top of it, a centrifuge and an old computer she said no one would miss if this didn't work out. "I gave it a series of simple commands to complete on each piece of equipment."

A circuit she'd plugged into the tablet-sized device started to glow. Red at first, then gold as it released chimeras of heat into the air. The color flowed along a series of wires and microchips she'd embedded in a viscous gel. "Should it be doing that?" he asked.

The device vibrated enough to dance across the table. The gel melted into a puddle of goo as the circuit burned white-hot and the water inside the beaker boiled with an instant fury before it bubbled over the top and the glass shattered.

"G!" She was already backing away when he ran to pull her to safety.

The fried circuit erupted with a tiny flame that had

fizzled out by the time Hud could grab the fire extinguisher to smother the burned-out device.

Gigi stared at the foam-covered mess for several seconds before she turned to her laptop and typed in some pertinent information. "Enough spark to light a cigarette, but not enough power to run a portable generator or guide a missile or even turn on my toaster. It never got past the first command before it burned itself out."

"Your boss's design is an epic fail."

"This is twice the size of what Ian designed, and it couldn't handle the power output. No way could this be miniaturized and get any usable results."

Hud pushed his goggles up on top of his head and nodded his agreement. "This is why someone killed him?"

"It's a great idea. But I can't imagine Ian being so far off in his calculations." Gigi linked her fingers with his and leaned against his arm. But then he felt her stiffen against his side. "Once Ian's killers realize this isn't worth the cost of the parts, what will they do to Tammy? To you? To me?"

He pressed a kiss to her temple, trying to soften the harsh reality of his words. "I don't imagine these people are going to say, *Nice try*, and go away."

"What if Ian told them it didn't work? Maybe that's why they killed him. And now they're coming after me because they think I can fix it."

Her eyes were distorted by the safety goggles when he turned to face her. He pulled them off her face and tucked them into the chest pocket of her lab coat. "Nobody's coming after you. You give them something tomorrow morning. Anything that looks convincing. And we'll arrest them. Once we know exactly who's behind this, we'll be able to poke holes in their story. By the time they figure out the formula doesn't work, they'll be fingerprinted and stuck in a jail cell." He touched his finger to the point of her chin. "Can you put together something like that?"

Gigi nodded.

His phone buzzed in his pocket. "It's Keir. I need to update him on where we are with this. Clean up what you need to, and let's get out of here."

Hud strode back to her office to answer his partner's call. He gave him the news about the failed experiment, and the fake version of Lombard's formula and design they were going to pass off to Lombard's killers and Gigi's blackmailers early tomorrow morning.

He watched Gigi through the glass windows as she put together another gadget that she could pass off as Ian's invention. After sticking that into her backpack, she wiped down the salvageable equipment and swept the rest into the trash. Then, almost as though she couldn't help herself, she pulled up a stool and sat at the table with her legal pad and started sketching something on the paper. She'd once told him that she was always thinking—with the one notable exception she'd confessed in the bathroom that morning. She was elegant and mesmerizing and powerful in her element. And yet she was vulnerable and brave—

"Earth to Kramer." Hud swore as he realized his distracted silence had left himself wide-open for the question he knew was coming. "I'll take that as a definite yes to falling for the damsel in distress?"

This wasn't like getting stood up by the woman whose honor he was defending in the alley behind a bar. "This is different, Keir. Even if nothing comes of this connection, I'm scared to death something's going to happen to her."

"But Hudson Kramer doesn't give up. You know she needs you right now."

What was that woman up to? Gigi was up again, pulling items out of cabinets, piecing something together he couldn't see from this angle. "I know."

"You love her."

"Gigi's waking up to her feelings and desires. I just happen to be the guy who's around to take advantage of that."

"Take advantage?" Concern crept into his partner's tone.

"Those aren't the right words. I'm lucky enough to be in the right place at the right time to reap the rewards. I'm her friend. But she's let me become more. She needs me to be more."

"You *do* love her."

Hud wasn't willing to admit that out loud. Somehow, saying the words made his feelings for Gigi that much more real. Saying the words would set him up for a world of hurt that he wasn't sure he could recover from when Gigi didn't need him anymore. "We have to keep her alive tomorrow when we make that delivery, Keir. Now get out of my head and get back to work."

AFTER VISITING TAMMY at the hospital and ensuring she would be fine recovering at the safe house, Gigi and Hud had driven home.

Who knew a man with such a strong German surname could put together a delicious pasta and salad for dinner? Although she appreciated his efforts to take care of her and keep her distracted from her worries about the looming six o'clock deadline, Gigi had picked at her salad and pasta Bolognese. They'd cleaned the kitchen together and cuddled on the couch to watch the end of the movie they'd cut short the night before. If these were normal circumstances, she would have considered this the perfect date night—like the ones she used to imagine but had never gotten to experience.

But these weren't normal circumstances. And no amount of action, snappy dialogue and a hint of romance could make her forget that. Although she relished the warmth of Hud's body snugging her to his side, she'd missed the movie's climactic rescue from the flooded building after a devastating earthquake.

"What'd you think?" Hud asked, trying to make conversation because he was probably worried about her.

"It was…fine."

"Fine?" He pressed a kiss to her temple. "Talk to me, G. I don't mind that you're quiet. But this is too quiet."

She was physically exhausted and emotionally drained. But her thoughts kept coming back to one thing. "I don't like being bait."

He lifted her onto his lap and tightened his arms around her. "I don't like it, either. But—"

"It's our only shot at getting these guys—I know." Gigi nestled her head against his shoulder. "Capturing the suspects in the act of acquiring the information they killed Ian for is the best way to connect them to his murder."

Hud nodded. "Right now, the evidence is all circumstantial. We can't get warrants to pursue specific leads until we can name a prime suspect. Then we can break their alibi for the time of the murder, search for weapons that match the wound and nail down the investigation."

"I know I'll be wired for sound and wearing a locator beacon in case we get separated. You and the rest of KCPD will be able to keep tabs on me. I say the code word and Keir and all your buddies will charge in to save me." She fingered the tiny button on Hud's collar. "I appreciate the logic and organization of all that. But I'm still scared."

He caught her hand and stilled its nervous twitching against his chest. "That means you're human. Being scared is what keeps your senses sharp. It's what helps you survive."

He didn't understand. "Yes, I'm worried about the danger tomorrow—the violence surrounding these two people is...cold... They seem to...enjoy it."

"But?"

Gigi wound her arm around his waist and hugged her thanks for his patience and perception with her. He *did* understand that there was more going on inside her head than fearing the danger of this operation.

"I'm scared to find out who these people are. It has to be someone close to me, someone I work with—someone I trust."

"And you're wondering what other mistakes you've made about people. Who else wants to hurt you? Or use you?"

She nodded. "I thought I was making progress. But I really don't understand people at all. How am I supposed to trust my instincts about who's good and who's not when I wasn't smart enough to see the threat that was around me?"

"You know you can trust me. Right?"

She nodded. But then she found herself wondering if even that was a mistake. This man had her heart. She'd given him her body and bared her insecurities to him. But was she mistaking desire and empathy for love? Every newfound instinct said Hudson Kramer was the man for her. She didn't believe he'd harm her in any way, or that he could be a part of Ian's murder. He'd been with her during the phone calls, after all. But Ian's killer *did* have a partner.

Gigi shifted uncomfortably in Hud's lap. No. Hud wasn't a killer. He was a cop. They were partners. He was the brawn to her brains.

But the seed of doubt had been planted. Even if he wasn't part of the murder and blackmail, what if he was simply getting close to her, using her, for his investigation? What if she was as wrong about Hud as she'd been about Gary or Evgeni, Hana, or whoever was responsible for Ian's death?

"You know, I can almost hear the wheels turning when you get stuck inside your head like this."

Hud gently stroked her back, stirring her from her thoughts.

Gigi squeezed her eyes shut. *Head or heart?* Which one did she trust? One had never failed her. It warned her to be cautious. The other required a huge leap of faith. *Head or heart?*

"Did you fall asleep?"

When his arms changed position, and she felt him move as though he was going to pick her up, Gigi scooted off his lap. "I don't think I can sleep tonight."

She stood so abruptly that he reached out to steady her and rose beside her. "You going to explain what's going on? Look, nothing has to happen tonight if you don't want it to." He glanced down at the sofa. "I can bunk out here if you'd be more comfortable on your own."

She needed to do something. She needed to busy her hands so she could get these horrible thoughts about the man she loved out of her head. "Do you like cobbler?" Gigi dashed to the kitchen and opened the pantry door. "I've got apples or a can of cherry pie filling."

"You're going to make me fat if you keep baking me all these goodies." He followed her into the kitchen, his eyes narrowed with a look that said he knew there was more than a sudden craving for something sweet going on here. "If you need something to take your mind off tomorrow morning, I do love cherry cobbler."

She hated this. She hated that she'd even considered doubting Hud in the first place. She hated that her logic had silenced what her heart was telling her. She'd always embraced her intellect, but now she hated it.

Suddenly, tomorrow morning didn't seem to be the most pressing problem she had.

And then she knew the answer. She knew how to regain her trust in her feelings. She spun around, stopping Hud in the middle of the kitchen. "I know how to solve Ian's formula. I can make it work." She unzipped her backpack and took out the mock-up of Ian's capacitor and set it on the table. "With a few adjustments, this will run half a city block. Do you want me to write the specifics down for you? I've even drawn a rudimentary design so you can replicate it. It would be worth millions of dollars to anyone who builds it and owns the patents."

His eyes sparked with anger, then grew surprisingly sad. "You *don't* trust me. After all we've been through..." He scraped his palm across his cheeks and jaw and muttered a curse. "No. I do not want the damn formula. I don't want you to give me anything. I am not the bad guy here."

She just offered him what the blackmailer wanted on a silver platter and he'd refused it. "Surely you can see the logic in my suspicion. You're in the perfect position to betray me. I've been blindly depending on you and falling in love, and I thought—"

"Falling in love?" He laughed, and it wasn't that sexy, manly sound she found so charming. That laugh grated with pain. "You think too damn much. Nobody's falling in love here."

"I was scared. You'd be the perfect infiltrator, the perfect weapon to use against me. You've been with me for the past forty-eight hours, going every place I go, watching everything I do. Once the idea got into my head, I had to ask." She tapped the side of her head. "I had to know up here. I'm sorry. You know I don't understand how people work."

"I thought you understood *me*. Thought you trusted me. That I'm here to protect you. That I…feel…for you. That I would never hurt you. I thought we were a team." He nodded toward the ingredients she'd set on the counter. "Go make your cobbler. This kitchen is no different than your lab—piecing together machinery, cooking up projects. Thinking about big ideas instead of dealing with real people because that's easy for you. Put your trust in your experiments, your equations, your mixing bowls. That's all you need—ideas and things. Stupid me. I was dumb enough to actually believe you needed me."

"You're not stupid. I never said—"

"It's time for me to check the perimeter of the house." He strode down the hallway. "Lock the door behind me."

"Hud." She'd hurt him by doubting him for even a moment, hurt him badly. There was no coming back from this mistake. There was no solution she could figure out on a whiteboard or her computer. "I'm sorry. I'm tired and I'm scared, and I don't know how to handle…us."

But he was out the door, walking to the front sidewalk, looking up and down the street. He walked to the fence and followed it until he disappeared by the back alley.

She was sprinkling the streusel topping on top of

the cherries and cake when she heard Hud's familiar knock at the front door. She slid the baking dish into the oven and hurried to the door to let him in.

"Everything's secure. I'm going to sack out on the couch for a couple hours before we have to get to the drop-off. I'll call Keir to keep an eye on the house while I'm asleep." Once she realized that was all the conversation she was going to get tonight, she returned to the kitchen to clean up her mess. She startled when she heard his voice from the kitchen table behind her. "Have you written down the formula anywhere? Is it on a flash drive or in a file folder?"

He held the capacitor in his hand, the design that re-created Ian's failed model from this afternoon. With his arms folded across his chest, and his muscles straining against the cotton of his shirt, he made a deceptively large figure in her kitchen. The anger was gone, but the tough guy was still there. This was Hud the detective, the man who'd promised to catch a killer and keep her safe.

"I sketched some of the details on my notepad. But most of it's still in my head."

"Keep it there." He handed her the capacitor. "You're sure this thing doesn't work?"

"It'll overheat and burn up just like the one I made this afternoon."

"Good. I don't want that formula getting into the wrong hands. As long as it only exists in that crazy headspace of yours, there's no reason for them to hurt you. The minute those details are in a form they have access to, you become expendable."

*Details.* She couldn't help it. With the way her brain was hardwired, she just couldn't help it.

Gigi ran to the sink. She set the capacitor on the counter beside it and pushed aside the curtain to look across the driveway to the house next door. "The details aren't right."

"With your formula?"

Her brain had skipped beyond that, putting together a puzzle she hadn't realized was bugging her until this very moment. "Outside."

Hud joined her at the window, peering out into the darkness. "Did you see someone?"

That was the problem. "Miss Allan. Look at how quiet her house is." His posture bristled with wariness. His instincts were telling him something was off, too. "I come home late. She's out her door in the middle of the night in her pajamas to check on me. Her dog barks and she's out before dawn to see a possum and meet the cute new guy next door. But a car blows up in the driveway—an ambulance, the police and the KCFD come—and she doesn't even turn on a light?" Gigi hugged her arms around her waist. "Said cute guy just walked through her side yard, and—"

"I get it." Hud looped his badge around his neck and headed to the front door.

Gigi hurried after him.

"Lock the door behind me." Hud paused to squeeze her shoulder. Reassurance? A reminder to heed his instructions? "Put your shoes on. Keep your phone in your hand in case something's wrong and we need to make a quick escape. I'll check on her."

She grabbed the sleeve of his flannel shirt when he stepped out on the porch. "Are we okay?"

"Not now, Gigi." He shrugged off her grip.

Gigi. Not G. Not the silly abbreviation that sounded like *darling* or *honey* or *sweetheart* to her. They were so not okay.

It hurt to see him walking away into the shadows—to see him distancing himself when they'd gotten so close. She was the stupid one. She'd chosen her head over her heart, and that decision might well have cost her any chance she had with Hud. Her heart was paying for that mistake.

She stepped away from the door and hurried to the side window to watch Hud knock on Kelly Allan's front door. No porch light came on. No light at her bedroom window. Gigi's heart sank with a kind of dread she was becoming far too familiar with.

When Hud jogged down the front steps and hurried around to the deck behind Miss Allan's house, Gigi grabbed her tennis shoes and backpack and ran back to the kitchen to watch until Hud disappeared behind the corner of her house. She put her shoes on and stuffed the listening equipment inside her bag along with Ian's flash drive and a printout of his notes. She'd be ready to go the moment Hud told her to.

She pushed aside the curtain to watch her neighbor's house.

Why weren't any lights coming on?

She squeezed the phone in her hand. Why wasn't Hud calling?

Two bright flashes suddenly lit up the black windows of Miss Allan's kitchen. A split second later, she heard the *pop, pop* of two gunshots.

"Hud!"

A third flash revealed the silhouette of a figure with an outstretched arm, aiming at the back door. It was only a momentary glimpse, but the flare at the end of the barrel and the muffled pop of gunfire were unmistakable.

"No!" Her breath locked up in her chest. Terror squeezed her heart.

She dropped the curtain and turned away from the window. What should she do? *Think!*

She was desperate to go over there. Hud said to stay put.

But he needed her. He could be hurt. Dying.

Her thumb automatically tapped 911.

Obey his orders? Take a chance?

Stick with the plan and catch a killer? Go to the man she loved?

A rapid knocking on her back door jolted her from her thoughts and she screamed.

Gigi glanced toward the front of the house and frowned. Hud always used the front door because the back door had been tampered with and was jammed shut. But the back door was closer to Miss Allan's house. If he was hurt...if he'd come to her for help... What if the shooter was in pursuit?

The harsh knock banged again.

When had she become a screamer?

Oh, hell. "Hud?"

She ran to the door. Unlatched the dead bolt. Un-

locked the knob. She pulled with all her strength, jim-
mying the spindle from the twisted strike plate.

The moment it started to give, it took a hard shove
from the other side and the door swung open.

Gigi stared into the barrel of a gun.

## Chapter Thirteen

Gigi retreated as the curvy figure, dressed in black, with a black stocking mask hiding the woman's face and hair, walked in, pointing the gun squarely at Gigi's heart.

"Stop." Even slightly winded, Gigi knew that voice. "Did you call the police?"

Had she completed the call? Was anybody listening in? She'd been so worried about Hud.

When she glanced down to see, the woman ripped Gigi's cell from her hand and threw it to the floor, crushing the screen beneath the heel of her boot before kicking it away.

"Why are you doing this, Doris?"

"Because you and your boyfriend have a trap planned for us. Who knew you had a backbone and wouldn't do as you were told? Change of plans. I'm not feeling six a.m. anymore. We're meeting right now." When Gigi continued backing away from the gun, Doris Lombard's arm snaked out to grab her, crushing five bruises into Gigi's upper arm, and a sixth one against her breast as she shoved the barrel of the gun into her chest. "Where is the formula?"

"There." She nodded toward the peninsula counter, not wanting to take her eyes off the gun or Doris's cold blue eyes. "In my backpack. Where's Hud? Is he dead?"

"My partner is dealing with him. I can handle you all by myself." Doris pinned her against the counter with her gun while she pulled the backpack toward her and unzipped it. "Did you make the corrections?"

Gigi wasn't surprised to hear the question. "You knew it wouldn't work. You gave me Ian's notes so I could fix the equation. So you could build a working capacitor and sell it or the plans to someone on the black market."

"Damn cop caught a piece of me." A second, taller figure, also dressed in black from head to toe, pushed his way in through the back door. He was tall, panting hard, clasping a gloved hand over his left shoulder, and annoyingly familiar. "Did you get it?"

Doris picked up the backpack. "She says it's in here."

"What did you do to Hud, Gary?" Gigi demanded.

Gary Haack glared down at her through the holes in his stocking mask. He tucked the gun he carried into his belt before turning over her backpack and dumping the contents onto the counter beside her. "Being too smart will get you killed this time, Professor Know-It-All."

"I don't have to be smart," she argued. "I could smell your noxious cologne all the way across the room."

Doris's gun pressed hard enough for Gigi to flinch. "She knows who we are. I told you we'd have to kill them both."

Tears stung Gigi's eyes. She blinked them away to keep her enemies in sight. "Hud is dead?"

"Two bullets will do that to a man," Gary joked. "He went down hard after that second shot." When he saw the tear trailing down her cheek, he reached over and traced it with his gloved fingertip. "Ahh, isn't that sweet. I thought maybe you didn't like men since you kept turning me down. But you really care about that cop." Gigi shied away from his repulsive caress. But she didn't get far because she bumped into Doris's gun on the other side.

The older blonde had peeled off her mask, giving Gigi a clear look at the displeasure curling her lips. "I'm going to hate killing you, Virginia. You were the only woman I ever trusted with Ian. I'll do you a favor and make it quick."

"Easy, babe," Gary warned. "You got a taste for blood when Ian backed out of our deal." Since his identity was no longer a secret, either, and they didn't intend to leave her alive to tell anyone, Gary pushed his stocking mask up onto his forehead. With one arm hanging uselessly down at his side, he reached for the bag he carried on his back, grimacing as he set it on the counter beside Gigi. He pulled out a small laptop and opened it. "We have to make sure she fixed the errors that Ian refused to. Let me have a look."

Was Gary smart enough to see the discrepancies in Ian's formula? Would fooling him by changing numbers and variables buy her a few more minutes of life? Was there any way she could escape these two greedy, vindictive murderers and make her way over to Miss Allan's house to see if Hud was still alive? To see if she could save him? If there was any chance she could tell him how grateful she was to him for coming into her life and teaching her about love?

"What about Miss Allan? Did you kill her, too?"

"Shut up," Gary muttered, rummaging through her things until he found the flash drive from Ian's safe. "Is this the formula?"

Gigi nodded.

"Which one?"

She gave him the file number and encryption code she'd added this afternoon at the lab. While he waited for the file to load, he picked up one of her notepads and skimmed through the diagrams she'd drawn. Hud had been right. The real formula would be in Gary's and Doris's hands right now if she'd written it down. But would Gary recognize the fake? Her glasses were fogging up with the heat of her tears, but she left them in place to mask the uncertainty in her eyes.

He tossed the pad aside as the file came up and he scrolled through it. "Oh, Gigi, Gigi, Gigi."

*You know you can't play me like this. Where is the real formula?*

She held her breath, expecting to hear the words, but they never came. Instead, he shut down the laptop and pocketed the drive. "Miss Allan invited us into her house and served us iced tea yesterday when we told her we were friends of yours and were concerned for your safety. Didn't recognize me from Friday night. Then that yappy dog of hers decided he didn't like me and wouldn't shut up. Made her suspicious. She tried to fight with me when I refused to leave. When I shoved her away, she hit her head on the counter."

A little more hope squeezed out of Gigi's heart. "You could have called an ambulance."

"Oh, wise up." He slung the bag over his shoulder. "Do you know how much the Lukin dissidents will pay for this? How much I can make once I put my name on the design and sell it? There's too much money at stake here—too much satisfaction at besting you and Lombard both—for me to have any regrets now."

"So you killed Ian for the money and professional jealousy. And you...?" She turned to Doris.

The older woman was getting antsy about chit-chatting, but she seemed pleased to share her motive for murder. "All those years Ian cheated on me, and that rat threatened to divorce me when he discovered my affair with Gary. Told me he'd rather destroy his formula than make the millions he promised so that I couldn't get a dime of it." Doris's nostrils flared as she drew in a breath, savoring it as if she was inhaling an intoxicating memory. "I stabbed him again and again, once for every woman I knew about."

Gigi supposed she should feel affronted that Gary had continually hit on her and even talked marriage while he was bedding his boss's wife. But frankly, she was glad she'd paid attention to the icky vibe she got off him and had steered clear of that relationship. Or maybe she should be sickened by Doris's lust for violent revenge.

Instead, she was focusing on the details. Analyzing the room and slyly studying the nuances of her captors, wondering if she had any chance of living through this, of seeing her sister again, of telling the police everything they'd just confessed to her. She wanted to go to Hud's funeral, to honor him, to thank him. She wanted to celebrate Kelly Allan's life, and Ian Lombard's. "How are you going to explain away all the dead bodies?"

"Why you, my dear." Gary packed up her notepads with his laptop and pulled his gun from his belt. "Brilliant scientist. Embarrassing social skills. Hold her," he said to Doris. The blonde moved her gun to Gigi's temple and grabbed her right wrist, forcing her arm up. Gary shoved his gun—the gun he'd used to shoot Hud—into her hand. Doris squeezed Gigi's fingers around the grip, leaving a set of fingerprints on it, before Gary pulled the gun away. He shoved her belongings into her backpack, along with the gun. "It will be easy to paint a picture of you cracking under the pressure to compete and achieve."

"I'm working with the police. They'll know that's a lie."

"Will they?" Doris joined the conversation. "Who did Ian trust with his secrets? Who took his formula and designs from the safe at my house?"

"Who left the Lukin reception early to meet Ian in his office?" Gary taunted. "I followed you out of the hotel. Would have offered you a lift, but I had other plans."

"That's not what happened. He left to meet with…" She looked at Doris's smiling face. "You."

"You were right, darling," Doris cooed, reaching up to brush a lock of hair off Gary's forehead, all without moving the gun aimed at Gigi's head. "She *is* a smart girl."

"You came back from your trip early," Gigi surmised. "Arranged some kind of late-night rendezvous with your husband. You both like the same whiskey. I bet you brought your own bottle. Drugged Jerome with your motion-sickness medication so he'd be passed out when the power went off in the lab." She glanced up at Gary, feeling her tears drying up and a whole lot of anger taking their place. Interesting how embracing her emotions could clear her head of debilitating thoughts and allow the details she needed to see to come into focus. "Nice job with that. Sneaking into Ian's office and programming the blackout."

"Your word against ours. And you'll be dead. The dissidents weren't happy you reneged on your deal with them."

The timer dinged on the oven, diverting Doris's and Gary's attention momentarily. "My cobbler is done." She touched the barrel of Doris's gun and nudged it aside. There were three college professors in this room, but only one of them was truly observant. "If you don't mind, I'd like to take it out of the oven. I'd hate for the house to burn down. It will be the only thing I have to leave my sister after I'm gone."

Gigi stepped away from the two of them. She needed to do this quickly before either of them got past the non sequitur of baking dessert when they'd been talking murder.

Keeping her back to Doris and Gary, she reached across the counter to pick up her oven mitts. As she pulled them on, she picked up the faulty capacitor and opened the oven door. She set the device inside, pulled out the baking dish and cranked the heat as high as it would go.

"What are you doing?" Doris reacted first. She grabbed a hunk of Gigi's hair and pulled her backward.

Gigi kept hold of the hot baking dish and swung around, smashing it in Doris's face. The glass shattered and the hot filling bubbled onto her skin and she recoiled, screaming.

"Doris!"

The ruthless blonde dropped her gun as she sank to her knees, cradling her burnt, battered face and moaning. Gigi snatched the mixing bowl off the counter and hurled it at Gary, forcing him to duck while she dived after Doris's gun.

But she'd miscalculated Gary's reach and her own clumsiness in shedding the oven mitts to pick up the weapon. He grabbed her by the neck and hauled her to her feet, kicking Doris's gun beyond her reach as he lifted her onto her toes.

"You think you're so damn clever?"

Gigi clawed at his hand, gasping for air, feeling the bones in her neck contract. He threw her against the stove, never loosing his one-handed grip on her—jarring her body, reminding her of the oven's rising heat.

"You don't get to win this time," he spat in her face, hurling her into the cabinets, cracking her elbow against the countertop and knocking utensils and measuring cups to the floor. She punched at the wound on his shoulder, but she was losing strength, losing consciousness. He slammed her onto the countertop, using his superior height to put even more pressure on her neck. She twisted, kicked. But her eyes were drifting out of focus. She opened her mouth, but no air seeped through his crushing grip. "Ian treated you like a goddess. Like you were the only one of us who mattered. His prize. I hate everything about you."

"Get your damn hands off her."

Hud's deep, drawling voice was pure predator.

His appearance at the back door was an unwelcome surprise to Gary. His stranglehold on her neck loosened. Air rushed into Gigi's lungs as joy rushed into her heart.

"Hud?" she croaked, her throat raw, her world spinning.

Gary turned as five feet eight inches of coiled dynamite launched himself. Hud hit the bigger man square in the stomach, folding him in half and knocking him off his feet. The two men landed hard. Her ears filled with thuds of fists against bone and grunts for breath and curses of pain.

"Hud?" Her body was bruised, every breath a raspy scratch through her throat. But oxygen was filling her lungs and her strength was returning. "Thank God… Not dead…"

Gary kicked Hud off him and Hud tripped over Doris's huddled form as she tried to crawl away from the fight. Then Gary was on top of him, hitting him in the gut.

"Hud!"

He howled in pain. Her relief at seeing him alive quickly waned when she saw the blood soaking his shirt and rolling down the side of his face. She swung her legs off the counter, wobbling when her feet hit the floor. *Two bullets will do that to a man.* The man she loved had been shot twice and left for dead. But he wasn't dead. Hudson Kramer was strong. He was a fighter. He was a miracle. He'd saved her life, just like he promised.

He was on top of Gary now, his meaty fist breaking Gary's glasses with one blow. But he was so pale. So hurt.

He needed her help. Where was Hud's gun? Doris's gun? Gary's?

Her bag. It had been knocked to the floor in her struggle with Gary. But if she could reach it... She shoved Doris out of the way and...froze.

Her nose stung with the acrid smell of burning chemicals. Oh, hell. The oven. They needed to be on the other side of that peninsula. Now. "Hud!"

Doris staggered to her feet, holding the edge of the sink so she could stand.

Gigi spotted the white-hot glow through the oven door.

"Hud!" She grabbed him by the shirt collar and dragged him off Gary. She pushed him toward the kitchen table and dove on top of him, crashing to the floor behind stools and cabinets. She wrapped her arms around his shoulders and rolled away from the open part of the kitchen as the oven exploded.

There was a whoosh like a freight train flying past and a horrible shriek. Glass shattered and shards of metal bit through wood cabinets.

"I've got you," she whispered against his ear as shrapnel rained down around them.

When the last of the debris had settled, Gigi pushed herself off Hud's chest. She heard moaning from the other side of the peninsula. People needed medical attention. She had to find a phone and call for help.

She realized that Hud's hands had latched on to her waist, holding on to her as tightly as she'd held on to him. His golden eyes searched her face with a fierce expression she didn't quite comprehend. "You…one piece?"

She nodded.

He was breathing irregularly, and she could feel the warmth of his blood soaking into her clothes from his wound. She was so afraid he was dying. She was so grateful he'd come back to her. There were far too many words that needed to be said.

So, she lowered her head and kissed him.

Then she pushed to her feet to see the damage that she'd done. Hud caught her hand and she helped him to his feet. "Need my gun." Between her and the counter, he braced himself and followed her around the peninsula. "Pretty boy took it off me."

"It's in my bag." She stooped down to retrieve it. "How badly are you hurt?"

"Not so bad I can't do my job." Hud checked the weapon before snapping it in the holster on his belt. "Help me with pretty boy."

Doris, who'd been hit by the oven door when it blasted off, was out cold. Hud picked up her weapon and tucked it into the back of his belt. Gary moaned from shrapnel cuts and his shoulder wound as Hud pulled his arms behind his back and cuffed him.

Then Hud sat, leaning back against her gouged and broken cabinets while Gigi grabbed two towels to stanch his wounds. He grimaced as she applied pressure to the hole in his side and the graze at the side of his head. His breathing was still off, his skin dotted with clammy perspiration. But his eyes locked on to hers as he took over holding the towel to his head wound. He nodded toward the oven. "What the hell was that?"

"Physics."

With his free hand, he pulled her to him to plant a hard, fast kiss to her lips. "Bless that beautiful brain of yours."

Gigi breathed a sigh of relief when she heard the first siren. It grew louder as the sounds of other emergency vehicles joined it.

"I called Keir before I stumbled over here. Cavalry's coming." He touched a finger to the point of her chin, asking for attention to his words, not his wounds. "What happened earlier. I overreacted. With my track record... We'll figure it out."

Hope blossomed with that promise. "I'm good at figuring out problems."

"Yes, you are."

"I'm sorry I doubted you. I was afraid I'd never get the chance to tell you I was wrong. I never meant to hurt you." Her sinuses burned as she held back tears. She was a one-man woman, and she'd nearly lost her chance with this brave wonderful man. "Gary said you were dead."

"Yeah. Well, thank God he's as bad a shot as he is boyfriend material." He glanced toward the graze that had mowed through his spiky hair. "This supposed kill shot was like a blow to the head. Knocked me out for a few minutes."

"Welcome to the concussion club."

He started to laugh but cursed instead. "Don't be

tellin' jokes, G. I think this one—" he touched the towel she held at his waist "—is going to need some surgery."

She burst into tears.

"Hey." He caught the first tear with the pad of his thumb and wiped it away. He caught the next one, and the next as her glasses fogged up and the tears rolled freely down her cheeks. "What's this?"

"You called me G."

At 6:01 a.m. the next day, Gigi knocked on the door to Hud's room at Saint Luke's Hospital.

Doris Lombard was under close guard in the ICU. Gary Haack had been stitched up and locked away in a holding cell until his arraignment. Tammy was at home with an off-duty Albert Logan, dog sitting Izzy, who was missing her late owner. Gigi's injuries were minor, although she felt beat-up and had been instructed to keep talking to a minimum until her throat had healed. She'd written a long statement about everything Gary and Doris had confessed and explained why she'd set off a makeshift bomb in her kitchen.

Then Keir had driven her back to the hospital himself, kissed her cheek and wished her luck.

*Luck?*

*You're the first woman Hud's been with who I think is worthy of him. He loves you, Gigi. Go get him.*

This was the going and getting.

Only, she wasn't exactly sure how she was supposed to do this.

"Come in."

Hud was awake. She'd been hoping she could watch him sleep for a while. Give herself more time to think.

"G, I know it's you. Keir texted me." He chuckled softly. "And you're the only one who'd hesitate to come see me." She stepped around the curtain and caught her breath as she found him sitting up against a stack of pillows on the bed. He needed a shave, but, other than the bruising around his left eye, the healthy color of his skin had returned. He had a bandage on his head, an IV in his hand and a blue hospital gown stretched tautly across his shoulders and chest. "I'm sorry I ever gave you reason to."

*Head or heart?*

Gigi's pulse quickened, but she knew the answer.

He'd come through surgery just fine, had received a blood transfusion and antibiotics and was expected to make a full recovery. Still, she wasn't sure if she could touch him yet, if she *should* touch him.

She stuck her hands in the pockets of her sweater, instead. "I've been thinking about us."

"Uh-oh."

She moved closer as the words tumbled out. "We don't need to have a lot in common to have a relationship. We complement each other. We balance each other's strengths. And when it comes right down to it, we do have some very important things in common— we're both good at our jobs, we love our families. Damn it, Hud, you wear your heart on your sleeve and I want to protect that. I didn't even understand what my heart was feeling until you showed me. And I..."

He pulled her hand from her pocket, and the familiar touch sent a tiny jolt of electricity through her, shorting out her nerves and leaving her with the clarity she needed to make sense.

Gigi turned her fingers into his palm, linking them together. "I'm sorry I ever doubted you, even for a moment. I don't want you just to make me feel safe. I want you to make me laugh. I want you to eat my cookies and bring me out of my shell and listen when I don't make sense to anybody else. I want you to help me understand my strength and believe in your own and never doubt that brains and brawn make an unbeatable team. I want you to kiss me every day and burn up my sheets at night. Or in the morning or whenever you decide you can't keep your hands off me. Because I want to put my hands on you, too. I want you to love me… Because I love you."

Hud tugged her onto the bed and pulled Gigi into his arms. "Works for me."

\* \* \* \* \*

*Look for the next book from* USA TODAY *bestselling author Julie Miller later in 2020, only from Harlequin Intrigue!*

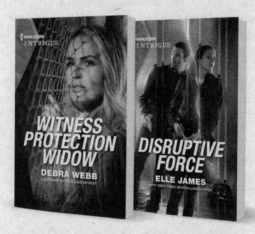

# COMING NEXT MONTH FROM

## H HARLEQUIN

# INTRIGUE

## Available April 21, 2020

### #1923 SECRET INVESTIGATION
*Tactical Crime Division* • by Elizabeth Heiter
When battle armor inexplicably fails and soldiers perish, the Tactical Crime Division springs into action. With the help of Petrov Armor CEO Leila Petrov, can undercover agent Davis Rogers discover secrets larger than anyone ever imagined?

### #1924 CONARD COUNTY JUSTICE
*Conard County: The Next Generation* • by Rachel Lee
Major Daniel Duke will do whatever it takes to catch his brother's killer, but Deputy Cat Jansen is worried that he'll hinder her investigation. As the stakes increase, they must learn to work together to find the murderer. If they can't, they could pay with their lives...

### #1925 WHAT SHE KNEW
*Rushing Creek Crime Spree* • by Barb Han
When a baby appears on navy SEAL Rylan Anderson's doorstep, he enlists old friend Amber Kent for help. But when the child is nearly abducted in Amber's care, they realize they must discover the truth behind the baby's identity in order to stop the people trying to kidnap her.

### #1926 BACKCOUNTRY ESCAPE
*A Badlands Cops Novel* • by Nicole Helm
Felicity Harrison is being framed for murder. Family friend Gage Wyatt vows to keep her safe until they find the real culprit, but there's a killer out there who doesn't just want Felicity framed—but silenced for good.

### #1927 THE HUNTING SEASON
by Janice Kay Johnson
After a string of murders connected to CPS social worker Lindsay Eagle's caseload is discovered, Detective Daniel Deperro is placed on protective detail. But Lindsay won't back down from the investigation, even as Daniel fears she's the next target. Will his twenty-four-hour protection enrage the killer further?

### #1928 MURDER IN THE SHALLOWS
by Debbie Herbert
When a routine patrol sets Bailey Covington on the trail of a serial killer, the reclusive park ranger joins forces with sheriff's deputy Dylan Armstrong. Bailey can't forgive Dylan's family for betraying her, but they'll have to trust each other to find two missing women before a murderer strikes again.

---

**YOU CAN FIND MORE INFORMATION ON UPCOMING HARLEQUIN TITLES, FREE EXCERPTS AND MORE AT HARLEQUIN.COM.**

HICNM0420

She wiped up stray crumbs, then tried to smile at him. "Coffee?"

"I've intruded too much."

She put a hand on her hip. "I might have thought so earlier, but I'm not feeling that way now. This is important. I give a damn about Larry, and now I give a damn about you. You might not want it, but I care. So quiet down. Coffee? Or something else?"

"A beer if you have another."

As it happened, she did. "I buy this so rarely that you're in luck."

"Then why did you buy it?"

"Larry," she answered simply.

For the first time, they shared a look of real understanding. The sense of connection warmed her.

She hadn't expected to feel this way, not when it came to Duke. Maybe it helped to realize he wasn't just a monolith of anger and unswaying determination.

As Cat returned to her seat, she said, "You put me off initially."

Another half smile from him. "I never would have guessed."

A laugh escaped her, brief but genuine. "I'm usually better at concealing my reactions to people. But there you were, looking like a battering ram. You sure looked hard and angry. Nothing about you made me want to get into a tussle."

He looked at the beer bottle he held. "Most people don't want to tangle with me. I can understand your reaction. I came through that door loaded for bear. Too much time to think on the way here, maybe."

"You looked like walking death," she told him frankly. "An icy-cold fury. Worse, in my opinion, than a heated rage. Scary."

"Comes with the territory," he said after a moment, then took a swig of his beer.

She could probably wonder until the cows came home exactly what he meant by that. Maybe it was better not to know.

*Don't miss*
Conard County Justice by Rachel Lee,
*available May 2020 wherever*
*Harlequin Intrigue books and ebooks are sold.*

Harlequin.com

HIEXP0420

# Get 4 FREE REWARDS!

## We'll send you 2 FREE Books plus 2 FREE Mystery Gifts.

**Harlequin Intrigue** books are action-packed stories that will keep you on the edge of your seat. Solve the crime and deliver justice at all costs.

FREE Value Over **$20**

---

**YES!** Please send me 2 FREE Harlequin Intrigue novels and my 2 FREE gifts (gifts are worth about $10 retail). After receiving them, if I don't wish to receive any more books, I can return the shipping statement marked "cancel." If I don't cancel, I will receive 6 brand-new novels every month and be billed just $4.99 each for the regular-print edition or $5.99 each for the larger-print edition in the U.S., or $5.74 each for the regular-print edition or $6.49 each for the larger-print edition in Canada. That's a savings of at least 12% off the cover price! It's quite a bargain! Shipping and handling is just 50¢ per book in the U.S. and $1.25 per book in Canada.* I understand that accepting the 2 free books and gifts places me under no obligation to buy anything. I can always return a shipment and cancel at any time. The free books and gifts are mine to keep no matter what I decide.

Choose one: ☐ **Harlequin Intrigue Regular-Print** (182/382 HDN GNXC)  ☐ **Harlequin Intrigue Larger-Print** (199/399 HDN GNXC)

Name (please print)

Address                                                                                          Apt. #

City                                    State/Province                          Zip/Postal Code

> ### Mail to the Reader Service:
> **IN U.S.A.:** P.O. Box 1341, Buffalo, NY 14240-8531
> **IN CANADA:** P.O. Box 603, Fort Erie, Ontario L2A 5X3

Want to try 2 free books from another series? Call 1-800-873-8635 or visit www.ReaderService.com.

---